THE BILLIONAIRE'S CONVENIENT BRIDE

THE BILLIONAIRE'S CONVENIENT BRIDE

LIZ FIELDING

MILLS & BOON

First published in Great Britain 2019
by Mills & Boon, an imprint of HarperCollins*Publishers*
1 London Bridge Street, London, SE1 9GF

Large Print edition 2019

ISBN: 978-0-263-08266-1

FSC
www.fsc.org
MIX
Paper from
responsible sources
FSC C007454

This book is produced from independently certified
FSC™ paper to ensure responsible forest management. For
more information visit www.harpercollins.co.uk/green.

Printed and bound in Great Britain
by CPI Group (UK) Ltd, Croydon, CR0 4YY

For my dearest daughter, Amy.
My rock.

CHAPTER ONE

Two cancellations for weekend craft class. Main boiler playing up. Rained all night. Need more buckets.

Agnès Prideaux's Journal

KAM FAULKNER LEANED FORWARD against the steering wheel, peering through the rain blanketing the creek to catch his first glimpse of Priddy Castle.

Just over a decade ago, he'd been an angry teenager looking back out of the window of the van containing all their possessions. Angry, afraid and desperately hoping for some signal, a last-minute reprieve, until the very last moment when the island had cut off the view of the only home he'd ever known.

Cutting off the last view of the girl who had caused all the trouble.

He'd sworn then, as the ferry had docked on

the far bank and his mother had forced a reassuring smile, a brave *Don't worry, we'll manage*, that he'd be back and he'd make her pay. He'd make them all pay.

It had been raining then. Not this soft stuff, little more than mist that clung to the windscreen, blurring the view. It had been drenching rain that had soaked their clothes as they'd stowed their home into a rented van.

It had run off Agnès Prideaux's long dark hair, down her face, her soaked T-shirt clinging to her as she stood on the quayside, watching the ferry leave. Saying nothing, not even a shouted sorry even though the loss of his mother's job, the loss of his home was all her fault.

The ferry cleared the island and his throat dried as he caught his first glimpse of his destination.

Castle was too grand a name for it.

Priddy wasn't one of those great grey fortresses built by the Normans. It had started life as little more than a stone watchtower thrown up to guard the entrance to the river and the once important trading port upstream from raiders, would-be invaders, its fortunes ebbing and waning like the tidal river it guarded.

It had been regularly abandoned, only remembered when new dangers threatened until an enterprising man, left in possession after some forgotten crisis, had decided to stay. He'd built himself a gentleman's residence alongside the tower, which became a decorative irrelevance until the eighteenth century when the risk of invasion from France gave it a renewed purpose.

The only invasion had been from smugglers carrying brandy and silk.

They slipped into the creek without challenge because Sir Arthur Draycott, baronet and magistrate, whose duty it was to guard the coast and hang smugglers, was in cahoots with Henri Prideaux, the most infamous smuggler in that part of the coast.

Not that Sir Arthur had lived to enjoy his ill-gotten gains. But his daughter had married the smuggler and Henri Prideaux had become king of the castle, his own title bought from equally corrupt politicians he'd done business with.

There was nothing to guard now and, with

the last baronet gambling away what remained of the fortune, Priddy Castle had become little more than an upmarket B & B.

He had wondered if it would look smaller than his imagination remembered but, looming out of the mist, the rain-darkened grey tower retained every bit of its threatening presence.

Chains clanked as the old pontoon ferry reached the slipway and the ramp was lowered. He forced himself to relax and joined the vehicles heading along the quay, past the row of old fishermen's cottages tucked in beneath the protection of the castle.

The fishermen had shaken off the shackles of the Prideaux estate when the railway had arrived on the far side of the creek, opening up the lucrative London market for their catch.

Artists, attracted by the light, and the cheap cost of living, had been drawn to the area until, around the turn of the century and it had become a well-known colony.

It had all been a bit ramshackle and scruffy when he'd left but today there were tubs of spring flowers, vivid against the freshly whitewashed walls, and an upmarket deli was doing brisk business serving the yachting fraternity that had grown up in the safety of the creek.

Even the old chandler's store, where he'd once conducted a lively back-door trade in the sea trout he'd poached from the creek, had been given a make-over.

The number of fishing boats heading out to sea might have dwindled to a handful, but tourism and the marina had filled the gap. The town of Castle Creek, with its pastel-painted cottages rising on the opposite bank in theatrical stages, had become a desirable place to have a holiday cottage. A place to bring your children for the summer. A place to build sandcastles on the beach, mess about in boats, build happy memories if you were among the privileged few.

Kam took the lane leading up to the castle, slowing as he rounded a bend, and then pulled over in front of the cottage that had once been his home.

Tied to his mother's job at the castle, the cottage had been neglected by a careless owner, but the windows had shone, the garden had been neat and cared for.

He'd seen photographs, but the reality shocked him. Roof tiles had slipped, there was a cracked pane stuffed with cardboard to keep out the weather. It was in the shelter of the hill, but paintwork needed constant attention this close to the sea. As for the garden. He would have to fight his way through the rank weeds to reach the front door.

If it was no use to the estate, why hadn't they sold it? Or done it up to let as a holiday rental. Things were bad now, but they hadn't always been.

After a moment to compose himself, he carried on up the hill.

On the sheltered, landward-side of the tower, the original house had been extended by successive generations until it had become a rambling muddle of styles, but as he swept through the gates it was the rose bricks of the Tudor frontage that appeared though the soft filter of the mist.

It looked better than he'd expected after seeing the cottage.

The gravel drive was weed-free and raked

and while the drifts of naturalised daffodils that would have lit up the long curve of the drive early in spring had died back, there were early tulips glowing pink through a haze of forget-me-nots in huge tubs by the heavy oak front door.

They did a good job of distracting the eye but, this close, the stains on the brickwork where the sagging gutter had overflowed during the heavy overnight rain were obvious.

There was an arrow pointing to the designated parking area where half a dozen cars were neatly lined up. He ignored it and parked near the front door. He grabbed his bag and, ignoring the damp mist that clung to his face, stood back to get a better look at the roof.

It wasn't only the guttering that needed urgent attention.

'Please, Jimmy…' Agnès Prideaux was beyond pride. She was begging. 'I did the jiggly thing that you showed me to get it going but it just juddered a bit. It needs your magic touch.'

'What that boiler needs is a one-way ticket to the scrapyard.'

'It's top of my list,' she assured him.

Along with patching up the roof, fixing the gutters and half a dozen other problems that her grandfather had ignored for years and then, having invested all the estate's disposable assets in a bank offering a high interest rate that anyone could see was a disaster waiting to happen, had drunk one bottle of brandy too many and died, leaving her to deal with the mess.

'If you could just pop over in your lunch hour and do your thing, I'll treat you to the chef's special in the conservatory.'

This was happening so regularly that she didn't need to mention the cash-in-hand payment that would come out of her own purse.

Jimmy sighed. 'I'm sorry, Agnès, but the boss has laid down the law. The castle is off-limits until your account is paid.'

'But—'

This morning had been a disaster. Without the boiler there would be no hot water for the guests after a long hard day creating their masterpieces.

'Even in my own time,' he added, before she could plead.

What?

'Can he do that?' she demanded as her struggle to maintain a swan-like calm while paddling frantically to keep ahead of her creditors, already stretched to breaking point, finally snapped. 'The miserable old goat knows he'll be paid as soon as the lawyers stop faffing around and settle the probate.'

She'd not only snapped but, far worse, she was lying. She was that desperate.

Probate had been granted a week ago but between her grandfather's lack of judgement and a looming inheritance tax bill, she was about to descend into negative equity in a big way. Her only chance of keeping the castle was to convince the bank that it was a viable business, but if the boiler wasn't fixed the comments on the review sites would ensure that there would be no more guests to feed the maintenance bills and the bank that liked to say yes would be saying not a chance…

'Can I speak to him?' she asked.

Another voice said, 'The miserable old goat has you on speaker phone, Miss Prideaux, and to answer your question, yes, if Jimmy wants to keep his job, he can.'

She swallowed. 'Mr Bridges—'

'Priddy Castle business is always welcome,' he said, cutting off her apology before she could even think how to recover the situation, 'but our terms are one month. We'll be happy to oblige just as soon as the outstanding account is settled.'

She held the phone to her ear for a long moment, but the connection had been cut. She'd been left hanging in space with nowhere to go.

'Problem?'

Agnès jumped at the unexpected sound and swung round on her chair.

The guests were all supposed to be safely out of earshot in the barn creating collages but the man leaning against the doorframe didn't look as if he spent his weekends messing about with scraps from the attic. At all. What was clear was that he'd been there long enough to have heard every word of her embarrassing conversation with the heating engineer.

She took a breath and did her best to arrange her face into a welcoming smile. 'Can I help you?'

'I have a reservation,' he said, 'but there's no one at the reception desk.'

'I'm so sorry. Suzanna must have been called away.'

'A complaint about the lack of hot water, perhaps?'

She felt the hot flush rush to her cheeks but rose to her feet, indicating with a gesture that he should lead the way. 'Are you here for the class?' she asked, reminding herself not to judge by appearances. He might want to tap into his creativity. 'It's already started but—'

'I haven't come here to upcycle rubbish into art.'

He hadn't used his fingers to make quote marks but the way he'd said 'art' he might as well have done. He had, however, paraphrased the poster pinned up on the wall behind her that listed the craft weekends she'd organised to bring in guests during the winter months.

His tone did suggest that he had something on his mind and her heart sank. Was this another of her grandfather's debts come to haunt them?

She cleared her throat to ask, since there was no use putting off bad news, but he beat her to the question.

'You don't recognise me, Agnès?'

Distracted by the crisis with the boiler, eyes gritty from scouring the accounts in a rob-Peter-to-pay-Paul attempt to find money for the outstanding plumbing bill—not to mention the eye-avoiding embarrassment—she hadn't given him much more than a glance. Total good hostess fail.

But then he said her name and a flicker of butterflies stirred beneath her waist.

He waited for her brain to catch up with what she had heard, what she was seeing.

A fuzz of the misty rain that had blanketed the creek since dawn clung to a familiar mop of unruly dark hair, olive skin…

The close cut beard was new but as she met the steady gaze of dark eyes, the years fell away, she was in her teens and in the desperate, painful throes of first love…

'Kam?' Agnès breathed the name, reached out to touch his jacket, as if to reassure herself that he was real. Curled back her fingers before they came into contact with the damp leather.

His beautiful boyish face had been battered into manhood, his shoulders had widened and the growth spurt that came later to boys had taken him past six feet. He seemed twice the size of the youth who'd been banished from the castle by her grandfather. Larger, tougher.

'Kam Faulkner,' she said.

'There,' he said, the corner of his mouth pulling up in the nearly smile that had stolen her heart the first time she'd seen him and, she discovered, still had the power to make it leap. 'That wasn't so difficult.'

Difficult enough. She'd been holding her breath and his name had been little more than a whisper.

'No…'

She was still holding it. Her chest hurt and she was feeling giddy…

If she hadn't been so distracted by the leaking

roof, the dodgy boiler, the fact that the castle was on the knife-edge of financial disaster, she would have known him despite the beard, the fact that his nose had been broken and a scar now ruined the symmetry of his brows.

Breathe…

'Breathe,' he said, catching her elbow as she grabbed for the back of her chair.

Easier said than done when the warmth of his palm, the touch of his fingers was sending shock waves through her body.

'Yes…sorry… I didn't expect… I wasn't thinking…' She made an effort to pull herself together. She should remove her arm. Touching was… 'It's been a long time,' she said, not wanting to think about what touching him had done.

A long time but eyes never changed. She had dreamed about those eyes. Dreamed about his hand taking hers. Wanting so much. Seeing that same want echoed back at her even as he stepped back, turned and walked away.

With an effort of will she removed her elbow from his hand and straightened, but as he took a step back she had to stop herself from reaching out, grabbing a handful of jacket to keep him close.

It was ridiculous. It had been years ago. She had been a teenager with a crush. But in all those years, the hideous school proms with a 'suitable' date, the marriage market debutant parties, no one had ever come close to that moment when he'd reached out a hand…

She swallowed, mouth dry, unable to think of anything appropriate to say.

How unexpected.

How wonderful to see him after all this time.

How disturbing to still feel the same knee-weakening desire…

That he'd reached out now meant nothing. It had been an automatic response when he'd thought she was going to fall. Nothing in his expression, in his manner suggested that this was a happy homecoming, that he was here to catch up with old friends. To catch up with her.

His smile had been fleeting, ironic rather than warm, his voice cool. And why wouldn't it be? She was the reason he and his mother had been banished from the castle, from their home. Which begged the question—why had he come back?

'How is your mother?' she asked, when the silence had stretched to breaking point. Desperately falling back on the conventional. Sounding like her grandmother talking to the youth who worked in the garden.

'It's a little late to be asking about my mother's health,' he said, giving her nothing back. Nothing to work with.

'She's—?' She left the question unasked. 'Grandfather…' Kam's face darkened. 'He died last year.'

'I heard.'

He didn't say he was sorry and his face was shadowed in the windowless little room. Unreadable. Not like the last time she'd seen him.

She'd raced to the quay desperate to tell him how sorry she was, to tell him that she'd begged her grandfather to change his mind, but she had been too late.

She'd tried to shout his name as his mother drove the van onto the ferry. The raw anger in the look he'd given her had dried the words in her mouth and she'd just stood there, a painful lump in her throat, helpless, hopeless, too miserable even to cry.

He'd learned to hide his feelings, but he had not forgotten.

Reminding herself that she was running a hotel, that he was a guest, she gathered a breath and dug deep for her professional smile.

'Well, it's lovely to see you after all this time. I hope you'll enjoy your stay.'

'I know I will. With or without hot water.'

There was a certainty in his reply, a suggestion that it had not been a passing fancy to stay at the castle.

'It will be sorted by this evening,' she said, with more confidence than she felt. 'Suzanna should be back at her desk by now. Would you like coffee? Tea? A sandwich,' she added a little desperately, when he didn't reply.

'Bacon?' he suggested, his mouth twisting in a parody of a smile as he reminded her of all the times she'd brought him her breakfast bacon in a sandwich. 'You offered the heating engineer lunch.'

She swallowed. He wanted lunch? With her? She didn't believe it for a minute and banished the butterflies.

'Jimmy is a lot more than a heating engineer, he's a boiler whisperer and I was asking him to surrender his lunch hour.' Clearly he'd heard every word and there was no point in pretending. 'Of course, if you know anything about boiler maintenance…?'

'I'll pay for my own lunch but reserve a table for two in the Orangery, Agnès, and I'll tell you exactly what I know.'

There was no upward inflection, no warmth to suggest this would be a cosy catch-up with an old friend but then Kam had never been cosy. He'd been a dangerous lad; she'd adored him on sight. As a three-year-old she couldn't do more than watch as he'd climbed trees where he could barely reach the branches.

She'd followed him relentlessly as a five-year-old, trying to copy him, wanting to catch fish and swim in the river, spend the night out in the hides he'd built to watch owls and badgers.

Wanting to be a boy like him. Taking no notice when he told her to clear off.

At six she'd cracked it with the bacon sandwich.

By the time she was fourteen she didn't want to be a boy but knew that if she went all girly on him he wouldn't want her around. But when she'd come home from school for the summer just before she'd turned sixteen, it hadn't just been her. The tension had been palpable. She'd expected him to be waiting for her that evening in the hide, but he hadn't been there, hadn't come. He'd looked and his eyes had said yes, but he'd kept his distance and she'd thought that because of who he was, who she was, she had to make the first move…

She'd got it so wrong. Even now, the thought of what had happened brought a hot flush to her cheek.

He had been dangerous then and he was dangerous now, to her peace of mind if nothing else. Every cell in her body warned her that he wasn't here on some sentimental pilgrimage. To relive his boyhood memories, the good ones before everything had gone splat. Whatever he wanted, she was pretty sure it wasn't a trip down memory lane.

Before she could make an excuse, tell him that she had meetings, Suzanna arrived at his shoulder and, making an apologetic face from behind his back, said, 'Mr Faulkner? I'm so sorry I wasn't in Reception when you arrived.' As he half turned to see who was talking to him, Agnès spotted the small bedraggled dog she was holding at arm's length to keep the mud from her uniform. 'I'm afraid Dora has been down by the lake.'

Down by the lake and rolling in duck poo from the smell.

'I'll take her while you show Mr Faulkner to his room,' Agnès said, tucking the dog firmly under her arm, glad of an excuse to escape, catch her breath.

'Would you like coffee, Mr Faulkner?' Suzanna asked.

'No. Thank you,' he replied, his voice noticeably warmer as he spoke to the receptionist, but he still hadn't moved, hadn't taken his eyes off her. 'One o'clock, Agnès,' he repeated.

Kam and his mother had been treated shamefully by her grandfather and he clearly had things he needed to get off his chest. Telling him that she was sorry would be meaningless but maybe hearing him out would help him draw a line under the past so that he, at least, could move on.

It would be painful, humiliating, but he deserved that courtesy from her.

'One o'clock,' she agreed. 'Suzanna, will you call Jamie and let him know? Mr Faulkner is a special guest,' she added, knowing that the chef would ensure that he offered them something a little more interesting than the basic fare. 'I'm sure Grandma will want to catch up with your news if you can spare the time, Kam,' she added, as if this were a perfectly normal social event, 'but if you'll excuse me, I need to give this little monster a bath.'

'It looks like the same dog,' he said, 'but it can't be Daisy.'

He remembered the name of her grandmother's dog? That should have reassured her but, on the contrary, it felt ominous.

'Daisy crossed the rainbow bridge years ago,'

she managed, through a throat that felt as if it were stuffed with straw. 'This is Dora. Her granddaughter,' she added, very conscious of Suzanna's interest. 'They have the same colouring, but she's smaller. The runt of the litter.' Desperate to escape his intense gaze, she turned to Suzanna. 'Where have you put Mr Faulkner, Suzanna?'

'He's booked into the Captain's Suite.'

'Oh.'

The suite had been named for the smuggler, Henri Prideaux. According to the legend on the castle website, he'd fallen in love with the daughter of Sir Arthur Draycott, baronet and local magistrate, charged by the Crown with the task of guarding the creek from those illegally running brandy and silk into the country. Sir Arthur, far from doing his duty, had been using his position to make a fortune as their accomplice.

Henri, so it was said, having fallen in love with Elizabeth, had given up his life of crime to marry her and settle down in Castle Creek.

It was the story she was using to sell the castle as a wedding venue. Take your vows in the pretty chapel where Henri and Elizabeth were wed, then seal your love in the four-poster bed where they created the Prideaux dynasty. She'd had a couple of enquiries, but if she didn't get the boiler sorted her big plans would be going nowhere.

'Well, you'll be comfortable,' she assured him, even while thinking that the Captain's Suite was an odd choice for a man on his own, assuming he was on his own.

Why was he here?

She made an effort to look no more than professionally interested but the corner of his mouth lifted in an ironic smile and she felt her cheeks grow hot.

She needed to focus…

The B & B, the wedding business, were her last chance to save the castle and the good news was that Kamal Faulkner had taken their most expensive room. Hooray! If her conscience was prodding her to offer it to him as her guest, she refused to listen.

If he wanted to indulge himself by sleeping in the Tudor four-poster, alone or with a partner, he would have to pay the going rate because she couldn't afford the gesture.

'How long are you staying, Kam?'

'As long as it takes.'

What?

Not her business. Her only interest was that he would be spending several days in their most expensive room. Whatever he might want from her, they would have extra money coming in.

Double hooray…

'Right… Well, if you need anything, Suzanna is here and will be happy to help.'

'What I want, Suzanna cannot give me, Agnès, but that will keep until lunch.'

CHAPTER TWO

Kam Faulkner is back, staying in the Captain's Suite 'for as long as it takes'. It? What can he possibly want? It had better be an apology because that's all I can afford.
Agnès Prideaux's Journal

AGNÈS SLUMPED AGAINST the door, hugging Dora to her as she shut it against anyone else who felt like wandering in and shaking up her world.

Kam Faulkner. She could hardly believe it.

Dora whined and wriggled and she set her down and sat at her desk to give her wobbly knees a moment to recover.

How many times had she dreamed of his return to Castle Creek? In her imagination it had always been a magical moment. He'd look, then do a double take as he saw that the skinny girl who'd once made a nuisance of herself trailing after him had become a desirable woman.

Okay, that was a fairy-tale fantasy straight out of a romance novel and she'd had those romantic fantasies drummed out of her long ago. Her grandfather would probably have beaten them out of her, but you didn't damage your only asset, the prize heifer.

Marriage was for duty, to bring wealth to the family, to provide heirs.

And forget desirable.

Her hair, caught up in an elastic band, was way off the shampoo-ad standard, she was wearing overalls and she hadn't stopped to put on make-up before her confrontation with the boiler.

She'd felt more like kicking it than sweet-talking the wretched thing but had been afraid it would give up altogether and die on her.

With all their guests hard at work in the barn, she'd felt safe enough coming straight to her office to call Jimmy.

Her heart might have leapt at the sight of Kam Faulkner as she'd realised who he was, but his summons to lunch hadn't sounded as if he was here for a friendly catch-up-with-the-family get-together.

The idea was ridiculous. Why would he give a tuppenny damn what had happened to her or her grandmother? Why would he want to set foot in Priddy Castle ever again, unless, heaven forbid, he was looking for some sort of compensation for his mother from her grandfather's estate?

Her mouth dried on the thought.

The fact that he'd chosen the Captain's Suite, her grandfather's old room, seemed somehow ominous—a statement of intent. She checked the computer for his booking and saw it was for single occupancy.

She squashed the stupid heart-lifting response, knowing full well that a romantic weekend to show a partner where he'd grown up would be much better news, because she suspected that whatever the purpose of Kam's visit, it did not bode well for what remained of the Prideaux family.

His mother was entitled, no doubt, but she

should have claimed for unfair dismissal when she was turned out of her home, lost her job, because of Agnès's grandfather's bigotry. Agnès's stupidity.

Now she would have to line up behind Her Majesty's Revenue and Customs, whose claim for inheritance tax was outranked only by the account for her grandfather's funeral and the legal expenses for probate.

Dora, clearly sensing her mood, gave her a sympathetic lick.

Agnès stroked a silky ear. There was no point going to meet trouble, it would come fast enough. 'Come on, you little monster. Let's get you cleaned up.' And then she would give the boiler another jiggle.

Kam Faulkner looked around at the room that had once been Sir Hugo Prideaux's bedroom, a room his mother had cleaned every day of her working life at Priddy Castle.

A room strictly out of bounds to the likes of him. Not that he'd ever obeyed rules, never let one keep him out of somewhere he wanted to go. He'd been in here before, when Sir Hugo Prideaux had been away up to his own kind of mischief. He knew that Lady Jane hadn't slept in here with her husband.

This part of the castle had been built in the sixteenth century and had diamond-pane windows, linen-fold panelling and an ancient four-poster bed with heavily embroidered drapes. He hoped the mattress was a little more recent.

He dropped his bag, tossed the old-fashioned room key on the dressing table and walked across to the window.

The sun, finally breaking through the mist, lit the froth of fresh, bright spring leaves of the trees in the castle woods, sparkled along the creek and off the hulls of the yachts moored in centre of the creek. His playground as a boy.

He'd known every nest, where to watch for badger cubs, wait quietly to hear a nightingale sing. He'd seen ospreys swoop for sea trout and dodged the warden to catch them himself without any fancy gear. There would have been a hefty fine if he'd been caught.

These days he could afford the rods and the

licence to fish legally but doubted there would be the same fun in it.

He turned back to the room, but it wasn't the impressive four-poster he was seeing. It was Agnès Prideaux's face as she'd recognised him. Something in those grey eyes before the shutters had come down and she'd been back in control and asking, oh, so politely after his mother.

That moment when she had seemed to lose her balance and he'd reached out and caught her arm. For a fraction of a second he'd had the feeling that all he had to do was draw her close, complete the circle, and his world would come right.

Imagination, he knew. If there had been anything it had been uncertainty, embarrassment, fear, because she knew his return could mean nothing good. Nothing good for her, anyway.

And there was absolutely nothing wrong with his world.

His phone pinged, a text from his PA demanding his attention, and he left the past to give his full attention to the present.

The future would wait until his lunch date with Agnès Prideaux.

* * *

Agnès washed and dried Dora, but when she took the dog back to her grandmother's room she was asleep in her armchair.

Agnès gently rubbed behind Dora's ear. 'It looks like it's just you, me and the boiler, sweetie.'

Dora gave a happy little yap as if she couldn't think of anything she'd like better, and the boiler, having had time to think about it, finally juddered into life.

She sagged with relief as the tension left her. The chances were that it would behave for a few days, but she urgently needed a heating system that didn't lurch from one crisis to another.

She needed a long-term solution and there was only one option left.

Showered, changed into the silk shirt and dark trouser suit she wore as her work uniform, Agnès stopped at Reception to let Suzanna know that they had hot water, at least for today.

'That's a relief,' she said, and meant it. Suzanna lived in and it wasn't only her job but her home that depended on the viability of the castle. She wasn't alone in that.

There were other staff who might not find work easily if she lost the castle, herself among them. And there was her grandmother. She had become increasingly frail and there was no money for care-home fees.

'Jamie is on top of your lunch. You won't be embarrassed in front of your friend,' Suzanna said, a question mark in the word 'friend'.

'He's… Kam's mother used to work at the castle.'

'Oh, right. So he's back to take a look at his old home…? Are you okay, Agnès?'

No, she was not okay. She was far from okay, but she said, 'I need some air after being stuck down in the boiler room.' Space to come to terms with what she had to do.

'Not a problem. Someone has to walk through the woods and check on the progress of the bluebells and it's not going to be me.'

Dora was at the door before Suzanna—who would do anything rather than step out of her high heels, pull on a pair of boots and walk a muddy path—handed her the pair of wellingtons kept behind the desk.

Once upon a time, back in the days when gardeners came in dozens and were paid a pittance, the castle gardens had been open to the public by request only. If you wanted to visit Lady Anne Prideaux's rose garden, you had to write and make an appointment.

Her great-grandfather had gone a little further, opening to the public on half a dozen days in the year when for a small sum—all in aid of charity—the castle servants would serve you with a cream tea in the Orangery.

It was what a gentleman did.

Her grandfather had needed hard cash and by then there wasn't a duke, marquis or earl who wasn't opening up his stately home to the public to help pay for the upkeep of their ancestral piles.

He'd opened up the gardens to the public for five days a week in the summer. It was, however, special flowers—the snowdrops, bluebells, azaleas—that drew the crowds in the spring. And then, in summer, Lady Anne's rose garden, planted in the early nineteenth century with roses brought back by a plant-hunting cousin from Persia, filled the air with scent and drew the crowds.

In the early days her grandmother had offered cream teas in the garden in good weather, in the Orangery in the colder, wetter months. Darjeeling, Orange Pekoe and Earl Grey, served in bone china. Scones, baked in the castle kitchen by the under cook, served with jams made from fruit grown in the kitchen garden.

Some people had come just for the tea.

Now they took in B & B guests, and lunches and afternoon tea in the Orangery were self-service from a counter. More practical, maybe, and no one walked off with the plastic spoons, but no one came just for the tea, either.

Aware that it would be colder under the trees, Agnès grabbed a jacket and scarf and paused at the door to breath in the fresh, damp air of an April morning.

Rainwater was dripping from guttering that needed replacing, but the sun had finally burned off the mist, a blackbird was singing in an oak tree and the sky was a clear pale blue. It was one of those perfect moments that needed savouring and Agnès closed her eyes and lifted her face to the light.

'Don't you have more important things to do than walk your grandmother's dog?'

Kam's caustic remark didn't faze her. He might have grown, become a man, but his footsteps were an echo through time. She'd heard him coming across the polished oak floor and steeled herself not to react as he came to a halt beside her.

The scent was new, though.

As a boy, Kam had been all about grass and newly caught fish in the summer, bonfires, sawn wood and wet dog in the winter. This Kam was a man, the scent still masculine but more sophisticated. Leather, good soap and something unfamiliar that stirred the butterflies back into life, sending a frisson of awareness across her skin.

She gave herself a mental shake. It was all memory, it wasn't real…

'I'm going to check the bluebell woods,' she said, briskly. 'Why don't you join me?'

'It's a bit early if you're hoping for a rush of visitors to pay for a new boiler.'

'It would take more than a rush,' she said. 'It would take an invasion.'

She risked a glance at him but he was looking out over the woods, his jaw set, his mouth a straight line. Whatever he was remembering it wasn't a recollection that brought him joy.

If that was how he felt, there was no point in putting it off until lunch. He might as well know the situation right now so that he could leave.

She cleared her throat and he turned to look at her. 'You wanted to say something?'

'Only that if you've come hoping to claim compensation from the estate for your mother, Kam, I'm afraid you're out of luck.'

His face remained stony, only the barest tightening of jaw muscles suggesting that she'd hit a nerve.

'We'll talk about why I'm here over lunch, Agnès.'

Then he looked at her and the butterflies stilled as she felt all his pent-up anger coming at her in waves. She didn't flinch. Years of living with her grandfather's temper had taught her to stand her ground and she was simply being honest with him.

'Why wait?' Whatever was on his mind would be easier said in the quiet of the woods than over dull food in the Orangery. 'If you come with me now you could at least avoid a mediocre lunch. You might even spot a badger.'

Something flickered in those dark eyes as he glanced away towards the woods. But then his head snapped round so that he was looking straight ahead.

'I have to meet someone.'

Who? Where?

'Maybe later,' she said, as Dora tugged impatiently at the lead. 'If you're staying that long.'

'I'm staying,' he said, turning to look down at her, eyes dark as pitch, his expression unreadable. 'I'm back for good.'

Before she could answer, could begin to think what that might mean, he stepped down onto the drive. There was a dark blue sports car parked casually alongside the front door that hadn't been there earlier and could only be his but he strode past it and headed down the drive.

Agnès stared after him, remembering the

jaunty walk, the cheeky smile of the boy she'd grown up with, the teenage Kam. There was nothing of that in Kam Faulkner's expression or in his determined stride, straight back and broad shoulders.

She wasn't sure she liked the man who'd returned but swallowed down a sense of loss. He owed her no smile. The debt was all on one side, but she'd have to wait to find out what he wanted from her.

Money?

His car must have cost telephone numbers and the way he'd ignored the guest car park and left it at the door, as if he owned the place, spoke volumes. He'd booked the most expensive suite in the hotel, her grandfather's old room, and the clothes he was wearing hadn't come from a chain store.

This wasn't a man looking for a few thousand pounds for his mother.

Maybe it was simply about returning to the scene of his banishment to show them all that the boy her grandfather had branded a half-Arab bastard had done more than survive. A lot more.

And she was glad. Truly.

That he was back for good, though, disturbed her.

Was he planning to buy one of those expensive places with river frontage, a boathouse, fishing rights? Rub all their noses in his success?

Everyone knew what had happened back then—you couldn't keep gossip like that quiet in a small town.

Would people remember, stop what they were saying when she went into the post office?

Did he still play the guitar?

The thought slipped into her mind without warning, a melancholy minor chord rippling through the woods at night as fresh in her memory as if she were leaning out of her bedroom window to catch the sound.

Dora's paws jiggled up and down in her eagerness to chase down the scents reaching her from the wood.

'Patience,' Agnès said, glancing back as she finally headed for the trees, but her disturbing visitor had vanished beyond the curve in the drive.

Where was he going? There was nowhere down the lane… Except his old home.

It had been empty for years. She'd suggested that her grandfather do it up as a holiday let to help with the running costs of the estate.

Fat chance.

Her grandfather had never listened to women and by the time he'd died there had been no money.

No money to fix the boiler, repair the roof, replace the guttering which, as the castle was listed, would have to be specially made to match the existing elaborate hoppers. No money to flip the cottage so that they could turn it into a holiday let…

She'd drawn up a five-year plan but it had ground to a halt. It was definitely time to look reality in the face and the woods had always been her favourite place to think.

Sunlight was filtering through the fresh green of the canopy but there was barely a hint of blue to lift her spirits and, as she took the path leading down to a clearing where the first bluebells would open, her footsteps beat out the word *trapped*, *trapped*, *trapped*…

* * *

Kam strode down the lane, oddly unsettled by his exchanges with Agnès. Her face, that last image of her, had been imprinted like a photograph on the hard drive of his memory.

In his head he'd known that she would be older, known exactly what kind of trouble she was in and yet the reality had been a shock.

In the few seconds when he'd watched her, before she'd known he was there, he'd seen the woman she had become. Her dark hair was still long and thick, tied back to keep it from her face.

Her voice was a little deeper, her shoulders wider, her neck still long.

But then she'd turned around to see who had invaded her privacy and he'd seen the dark shadows beneath eyes the exact grey of an osprey's feather lit by sunlight, the strain of constantly flirting with the edge of disaster as she attempted to keep Priddy Castle ticking over.

The heat of embarrassment at being overheard begging.

In the millisecond of shock as she'd realised who he was, before the shutters had come down and she'd retreated behind the façade of businesswoman, he'd seen something else. A flash of some unreadable emotion as memory had flooded in.

He would have given a lot to know what she'd been thinking at that moment, but she was no longer the girl whose every thought had been telegraphed in a look. She'd grown up and learned to hide her feelings.

There had been a wish to see her suffer but, as he pushed open the gate of the house where he and his mother had had lived, it occurred to him that in taking the castle from her, he might be doing her a favour. That it would be something of a Pyrrhic victory.

Except that he would own the castle and she would be the one pushed out into the world, having to reinvent herself, make a new life.

That would be justice of a kind, he told himself as he walked around the outside of the cottage.

There were more tiles missing from the rear of the roof, cracked window panes held together with tape, a broken downpipe.

In the back garden, half buried in dead leaves

and weeds, he found the stone under which he'd hidden his door key on the morning they'd left, because one day, he'd sworn, he would be back.

He turned it over, woodlice panicked and ran in every direction, a fat slug shrank from the sudden exposure to light, but the key was still there, waiting for him.

He picked it up, wiped it clean in the grass, dried it with his thumb. The lock was stiff but eventually turned and he stepped into the kitchen.

Technically, he was trespassing, but it was obvious that no one had been here in a long time.

Nothing had changed.

The kitchen hadn't been updated since the cottage had been built when Victoria was on the throne. There were shelves lined with paper that had rotted to shreds, a stone sink that was still fitted with a pump to the well, although mains water had been connected a century ago.

What was new was the smell.

Damp, mice, rot…

Everything was covered in a thick layer of dust, dried leaves had found their way in through the gaps under the doors, dead insects lay on the windowsills.

There was the same threadbare carpet in the living room and on the stairs, only now it was damp and mouldy.

He instinctively avoided the loose stair, the places that creaked as he walked upstairs.

The old claw-footed bath, worn with age but once polished to a shine, was streaked with limescale where a tap had been left dripping until someone had had the sense to turn off the water. He knew it must have been Agnès.

The brass fittings were green with verdigris and there were dead leaves and heaven knew what else clumped in a filthy mess in the bottom.

The rose-patterned wallpaper in what had been his mother's room was peeling from the wall, there was a puddle of water rotting the floorboards where a window no longer fitted and everywhere there were mouse droppings.

It would all have to be ripped out, taken back to the bare bones. Or maybe he should just leave it and offer it to Agnès and her grandmother. They'd need somewhere to go, there would be a vacancy for a housekeeper and Agnès would need a job…

They would be the ones begging him to fix the roof, the windows. Priddy pride brought low, he thought. Although it had been pretty low when she was offering the heating engineer lunch to come and fix her boiler and no doubt a bung his boss would know nothing about.

There was a fly buzzing in the window. The wood was swollen; he had to bang on the frame with the heel of his hand to open it so that it could escape. Outside the air was fresh and he leaned on the sill to breathe in the scent of the woods. He could hear the birds, identifying their calls with ease, and in the distance the faint clang of rope against mast out on the creek.

He could have been fifteen again. Foraging for mushrooms at dawn, his dog at his side. Catching a sea trout or two if the warden was safely out of the way to drop off at the chandler's on his way to school. At dusk he'd be lying in wait by a badger's sett, or watching foxes slinking through the undergrowth hunting for small mammals. He'd built a hide so that he could watch a pair of owls floating silently to and from their nest as they fed their young, Agnès holding her breath at his side.

He'd caught fish for a young osprey he'd found with a broken wing and even when it was healed and she'd found a mate, had young to feed, she still came to his whistle, sure of a reward.

He'd had that freedom snatched away from him to be replaced by the concrete confines of a city tower block.

He took a step back from the window but as he reached for the catch a movement on the path through the woods caught his attention.

Agnès with that ridiculous dachshund.

She stopped for a moment to take a photograph with her phone, the dog dancing around her. She was looking down, untangling the lead from her legs and then, as if sensing him there, she looked up, lifting her hand to shade her eyes from a low shaft of sunlight that sliced through the trees and lit her face.

How many times had he seen her do that? Make exactly that gesture, looking up at his window, hoping he'd be there, desperate for company, for freedom from the miserable atmosphere in the castle.

A little girl racing through the woods, calling his name, hair flying, all legs and arms, her eyes and mouth too big for her face. Tripping over tree roots, grazing her knees, having to be taken home to have them cleaned up by his mother.

A nuisance, a liability, a responsibility.

But she'd stopped falling over, started to bring food with her. Sandwiches, pie, cake.

She'd been lonely and he'd always been hungry so he'd tolerated her presence. More than tolerated—he'd made her his accomplice. He might have suspected, but the fish warden wouldn't dare stop Sir Hugo Prideaux's granddaughter to check her pink backpack for poached fish, not if he valued his job.

He'd taught her to swim, but only because she'd followed him into the river and he would have got the blame if she'd drowned. She could climb trees, knew to keep quiet in a hide; he'd even trained Ozzie to come to her.

He'd treated her like a boy. She was never girly, didn't care about getting dirty, tearing her clothes. But then one summer she'd come home from school and everything was different. She still came to the woods but her hair was no longer an untidy tangle; it was a dark skein of silk that he wanted to touch. And under the baggy T-shirts and jeans there was no hiding the fact that she was a girl.

He was older, but she was suddenly the grown-up and he felt awkward around her. Worse than awkward. Looking at her mouth made him feel weird, then interested, and he didn't know what to do.

His mother noticed—she noticed everything—and warned him to keep his distance. Agnès was growing up and Sir Hugo wouldn't want his granddaughter being touched by the likes of him.

Except she didn't stay away. He closed his fist at the memory of the river water running off her skin, gleaming pale in the moonlight. His hand running over the sleek softness…

For a moment their eyes met across the distance. Was she remembering that moment? That one forbidden touch?

For a moment it was as if they were frozen

in that look but then, as Dora barked, setting up a flurry of collared doves, she turned away and melted into the shade. And he was the one holding his breath. Responding to the memory like a green boy.

He'd wanted to look her in the face as he took everything from her, but he should have left it to his lawyer. It wasn't too late. This could wait. He could cancel the appointment with the architect he'd asked to meet him here and be gone before she returned from her walk.

He shut the window and, phone in his hand, took one last glance around the room, the patch of damp beneath the window, the darker rectangles on the walls where he'd stuck up posters…

He found the number but then hesitated.

There were things he wanted to see, plans he needed to make, and he still wanted to look Agnès Prideaux in the eye when he told her that he would have her castle, one way or another. But he wouldn't be indulging a need for pay-back by offering her the cottage.

He'd thought he had what had happened slotted away tidily in the part of his brain labelled

'The Past'. This was now, and he was the one in control.

He should have remembered that the first casualty in any campaign was the plan. He'd planned to be cold, clinical, detached. Instead he'd been swamped by the rush of memories of a time when they had been friends, allies, accomplices; of that first explosion of sexual awareness.

Agnès might not have a title but while she stayed here people would always think of her, treat her, as a lady. She might look worn down by the financial struggle she faced, broke, but that was the gentry for you.

He paid his bills on time, but until he gave the estate a new purpose, new meaning, to the locals she would still be Miss Prideaux, while he would be the boy whose father had disappeared one day, without a word, leaving his mother to scrub the floors at Priddy Castle.

CHAPTER THREE

Kam went to see his old home. Of course he did. I wish he hadn't seen it in that state. More to the point, how did he get in?
Agnès Prideaux's Journal

AGNÈS AVOIDED THE Orangery restaurant whenever possible. She had no control of what happened there and every time she was faced with the reality, she raged at the lost opportunity.

Everyone at the castle had pitched in to repaint the wrought-iron work, shine up the glass, make it sparkle. In her desperation to get it up and running so that visitors would be able to make a day of their visit to the gardens, come just for a lunch or tea, she had let them down.

She sighed. From the outside it looked pretty under a sky that had cleared to a clear pale blue, with the entrance flanked by two of the tubs of orange tulips that she'd planted up in the autumn. The colour offended her but she'd softened the effect with white forget-me-nots.

Once inside she could see that Suzanna had passed on the message and ensured that this wouldn't be a bog-standard lunch.

A table, half hidden by a vast palm that had only survived because it had, long since, broken through its pot, the tiles, and become rooted where it stood, had been laid with a cloth, linen napkins and silver cutlery from the castle. There was a spray of wintersweet in a specimen vase and a carafe of iced water.

The chef, employed by the caterers and as depressed at the heat-and-serve food he was forced to produce as she was, appeared briefly to reassure her that there would be something a little bit less motorway café for her guest.

'And no queuing at the counter. I'll serve you.'

'Thank you, Jamie.'

She was picking a few untidy leaves off a couple of small orange trees, when Kam pushed open the door, letting in a little whiffle of breeze that raised gooseflesh on her arms. It had to be the breeze.

'We're in the corner,' she said as he joined her. 'I'll be right with you.'

He made no move to sit and wait for her, but looked around, taking in the caterer's Day-glo-bright branding.

'Is this the best you could do, Agnès?'

She rubbed some aphids off a leaf before forcing herself to look up.

'I… There was a misunderstanding.'

'Yours or theirs?'

'Mine.' There was no one else to blame. 'Grandma had just had her hip replaced and I wasn't paying as close attention to the details as I should have.' And having had the reality of her situation laid out in black and white by the lawyers, she'd panicked. 'I didn't have the capital to install a kitchen that would pass the local authority's hygiene inspection.' She lifted her shoulders in what she hoped was a casual shrug. 'You have no idea how expensive a kitchen can be.'

'Couldn't you have got a business loan?'

'When I talked to the business adviser at the bank, he suggested I might be better off leasing the Orangery to professional caterers. That way I wouldn't have to worry about a thing.'

'Don't tell me, he put you in touch with someone he knew. What on earth were you thinking?'

She lifted her shoulders in an awkward little shrug. 'If I'd been thinking I'd have asked a lot more questions but this way didn't cost me anything.'

'What's the deal?'

She looked at him. 'Does it matter?' She'd had a vision of white wrought-iron tables, chair cushions in a vibrant jungle print, tall plants everywhere giving a green, quiet atmosphere. She'd talk about home-made soup and bread, food prepared on the premises using fresh produce from the castle garden.

The woman she'd had that conversation with had agreed that it would be charming and when they'd shaken hands she'd thought it was a done deal. And then reality had caught up with her.

'I signed on the dotted line, Kam, and I'm stuck with this for the next five years. The orange plastic, the canned soup, frozen mass-produced food, cotton-wool bread and all.'

'I saw the comments on the review sites.'

She pulled a face. 'The gardens are great but take a picnic because the restaurant is a rip-off.'

Her complaints to the company had been received with a shrug. This was their brand.

'How much are they paying you?'

'A percentage of the profits once they recoup their outlay.'

His face gave nothing away but she knew what he must be thinking. What an idiot…

She lifted her shoulders in a helpless shrug. He was right.

'I was totally naïve,' she admitted. 'Obviously creative accounting will prove that they never make a profit but at the time I was just so grateful to have something taken out of my hands.'

'You aren't the first and won't be the last.'

'No. Not that it's much comfort. I had hoped to be able to use this for weddings at the castle. Obviously I have to clear it out and hire in suitable tables and chairs, screens to block off the self-service area, but on top of that the caterers expect me to pay them to hire their space, to use their kitchen.'

She expected him to suggest legal advice. It

was what everyone had advised. But all he said was, 'At least you have orange trees. I'm sure they'll grow in time. You were always passionate about plants. You knew all the names of the wildflowers. Red campion, meadowsweet, ragged robin—'

'You knew which berries and mushrooms not to touch,' she said, cutting off the list of names her mother had taught her.

'That was self-preservation,' he said. 'I was eating them.' He nodded at the small mop-headed trees. 'Will these ever have actual oranges on them?'

'I hope so. They're small, but they were cheap in the post-Christmas sale at Wicken's Nursery,' she said, 'and I thought, with a bit of TLC, they'd add a bit of—'

Class. Add a bit of class. That was what she had been going to say but was afraid that he'd just mock her foolish pretensions.

'Be a distraction from the cheap self-service cafeteria vibe?' Kam suggested, filling the gap and mocking her anyway. 'And you may be right about the oranges,' he continued, which was just as well as her own tongue appeared to be stuck to the roof of her mouth.

He bent to take a closer look and every nerve jumped as his shoulder brushed against her arm.

'You've got a few buds here.'

She focussed on the spray of small white buds. They were the same shape as the drops on her mother's pearl earrings when she'd bent to kiss her goodnight, then say, 'Sleep tight. See you in the morning, sweetpea…' before leaving for the party from which she and her father never returned.

She swallowed to moisten her dry throat. 'The baby fruit will probably drop.'

'Will it?' For a moment neither of them spoke and, unable to help herself, she glanced up to find him watching her intently. 'I thought you were going to follow in your mother's footsteps.'

Her mother had been a horticultural student who'd met her father when she had come to spend the summer doing work experience in the rose garden.

She'd once overheard her grandfather complaining to her grandmother that it had been the most expensive cheap labour he'd ever had the misfortune to employ. Her father was supposed to marry a girl with an inheritance; someone who could boost the coffers.

A pretty tenant farmer's daughter was good for a roll in the hay but marriage was far too important to be complicated by emotion.

And the stupid cow hadn't even had the class to drop a boy.

'Shall we sit down?'

She didn't wait for a response but dropped the leaves she'd picked off the trees in a nearby bin and headed for their table. His long legs beat her to it and he drew out a chair for her.

'Thank you.'

He glanced across to where people were queueing with trays, eyebrow raised. 'Shall I go to the counter or will you?'

'Sit down, Kam,' she said, hooking her bag over her chair and nodding to one of the staff to indicate that they were ready to be served. 'The chef cooks and freezes dishes which I reheat in the evening for the craft workshop guests. We had a couple of cancellations so you're in luck.'

'So I'll get the same meal this evening?'

'Sorry, we're a B & B. Bed and breakfast. We only cater for the workshop groups in the evening because that's a package. It's not too late to sign up.'

'Would I have to actually take part?'

'It's compulsory,' she said, risking a smile.

'Then I'll go to the pub.'

'Good plan. You'll probably meet some old friends.'

He frowned. 'Aren't you missing a trick here? People pay good money to spend a night in a castle, dine with the gentry. Full silver services, antique crystal and Lady Jane playing the gracious hostess at the head of the table.'

Another unticked box on her plan to make the castle pay its way but she'd exposed herself to enough ridicule.

'We had to let the butler go,' she said.

'Before you were born. You could hire one for the night.'

'Is that what you came here for, Kam?' she asked, tired of playing games. 'To be waited on by me?'

'No, Agnès. I'm not interested in playing at this. I want Priddy Castle.'

For a moment she didn't think she'd heard right, then, as the words lined up in her head, she said, 'The castle? That's it? That's why you're here?'

'I'm about to make you an offer you can't refuse.' And he named the exact figure of the probate valuation of the estate.

For a moment Agnès stared at him and then she laughed.

Not a *Ha, ha, ha, you must be joking* laugh. It was a choked sound, torn from somewhere deep inside her.

Anger lit dangerous sparks of lightning, flashes of gold in the dark depths of Kam's eyes. 'No doubt you think it's on the low side. The probate valuation does not take into account the possibility of planning permission for development, but then I have no intention of building on the site and, as you are obviously aware, the castle, and other properties on the estate, will require extensive renovation.'

His home. He was talking about his home.

She had to explain, but before she could speak the chef was beside them, placing a dish before her, and then before Kam.

'Carpaccio of salmon wi' herbs and lime.'

It took her a moment to recover and say, 'Thank you, Jamie. It looks delicious.'

He frowned, then glanced at Kam as he picked up the carafe of water. 'If ye need anything,' he said, filling her glass, 'just gi' a shout.'

'I'm sure we have everything we need.'

'Aye, well, I'm here if ye need me.' He glared at Kam, pointedly ignoring his glass as he replaced the carafe on the table, then walked away.

'You may not be happy with your caterer, Agnès, but their chef is very protective.' He filled his own glass. 'Or is that possessive?'

'What? Jamie…' Oh, for heaven's sake. 'Kam, I'm sorry but I wasn't laughing at you.'

'Weren't you?'

'No—'

'No doubt you're wondering where I'd get that kind of money.'

'To be honest, yes.' Kam had been dragged

out of school just before his exams, gone who knew where and he was talking about a huge sum. It wasn't just the castle, the cottage. There were outbuildings, gardens, woods, land that stretched out as far as the coast. Everything on this side of the creek for a mile in either direction. 'I was hoping that you might give me a few tips.'

'When I write the book,' he said, shaking out his napkin, picking up his fork, 'you can buy a copy.'

For a moment, just a moment, she'd thought they were beginning to get past his anger, but that was a clear slap in the face.

'You've told me what you want, Kam, and, for a whole heap of reasons, mostly involved an ancient entail that I'm not going to go into, you can't have it. There is nothing more to discuss.' She tossed her napkin on the table and got to her feet and slung her bag over her shoulder. 'This meeting is over.'

She didn't wait for his response. Angry, amused, baffled, she didn't care. But her legs were shaking as she left the Orangery, first walking quickly then running to her car.

She called Suzanna from the ferry to let her know that she wouldn't be back until late and to warn her that Kamal Faulkner would not be staying after all.

Kam rose, instinctively, to go after her but found his way blocked by the chef. He wasn't actually brandishing a knife and Kam stood nearly half a head taller, but he was a wiry Scot and he raised a warning finger in his face.

'I don't know who ye are, pal,' he said, his voice a low growl, 'and I care less, but Agnès Prideaux is a lady and if ye know what's good for ye, ye'll remember that.'

The man's protectiveness, irritating though it was, had a fierce gallantry that Kam admired. Resisting the urge to push past him and go after Agnès, he stood his ground, not backing away but moving into the threat of that accusing finger.

'I've known Agnès since she was in her pram,' he said, softly. 'I taught her to swim, to fish, to be so still that a blackbird would take a worm from her hand. I knew her long before she was a lady, so step aside, Chef, and let me go after her.'

'I think she made it plain that she's had enough of ye,' he replied.

'Unfortunately, she doesn't have that option. This is business.'

He waited and after ten long seconds, Jamie stepped back.

That was the easy one. Agnès, he had discovered, was not going down without a fight.

So, where would she have gone? Back to the castle, hiding behind her office door? Or would she find some quiet corner in the woods or the garden to contemplate the reality of her future?

She'd taken over an old greenhouse built against the wall of the kitchen garden when she was about ten, and made it her private place. He'd helped her clean it and replace putty where the panes were loose. She was, she'd said, going to create a new rose and name it after her mother.

He went there first.

Inside it was clean, all her tools neatly held in clips. An old chair with a leather seat and wide wooden arms was still at the far end, half hidden by some large evergreen plant in a large pot. The little camping gas stove Agnès had bought at a jumble sale and used to make tea from the mint and lemon balm she grew in large terracotta pots was still there, as was a kettle and a clean mug.

The once rickety wooden trolley that she'd found in an attic and he'd fixed for her held a stack of notebooks fastened with elastic bands and, on the staging, there were pots filled with the roses she grew from seed taken from the old roses in Lady Anne's garden.

She used to hand pollinate the flowers, putting tiny labels on each one. She was still doing it. She had been passionate about breeding new varieties. Apparently she still was.

'What are you doing in here?'

He turned to find himself being watched by a young man.

'Remembering,' he said. 'Who are you?'

'I'm Tim. I cut the grass. It doesn't mind,' he added.

'I used to the cut the grass here,' he said. When his father had left, Sir Hugo had told him to get on with it. 'Does Miss Prideaux pay you?' he asked. 'Agnès,' he added when the young man looked confused.

'Agnès paid me the minimum wage when I started working for her. It's the law.'

'And now?'

'After a month she gave me a rise because I love the garden so much that I make it happy.'

'I'm glad to hear it.' All he'd ever got from Sir Hugo was a mouthful of abuse if he didn't keep it short enough. 'You're doing a great job, Tim. I'm Kam, by the way,' he said, offering his hand.

Tim backed away. 'I have to do something. You should come out of there. No one is allowed in Miss Agnès's greenhouse.'

'I hoped she be here,' he said.

'She's gone.'

'Gone?'

'I heard her car. It's the same car that Lady Jane used to drive.'

'I remember.'

'It's a classic,' Tim said, seriously.

'Yes, it is.'

He wondered who kept it running.

He stepped out of the greenhouse, closing the

door behind him, and Tim followed him out of the walled garden just to be sure he left.

Suzanna was in Reception. 'Do you know when Agnès will be back?'

'Not until late. Is there anything I can do for you, Mr Faulkner?'

'No,' he said, then, changing his mind, 'Is the dinghy in the cave?'

'Dinghy?'

'Small wooden boat with oars. I thought I'd go over to the island.'

'I'm sorry but that's off-limits to guests. There used to be a pretty summer house where the family had picnics, but it was ruined in a storm. There are some pictures in the library. The women in long white dresses, the men wearing straw boaters.'

'I'll take a look later,' he said, as if he hadn't seen them years ago on his 'off-limits' illicit wanderings through the house. He hadn't taken anything, touched anything. He'd just wanted to look, see what made these people think they were so special.

To see Agnès's other world.

He'd imagined her bedroom would be pink

and princessy, but it was not so different from his. It was bigger, but the bed was an old iron bedstead, the wallpaper had been put up half a century before and she had a decrepit old arm-chair in what he now knew was called 'country house condition'.

Unlike him she hadn't put up posters of musicians. Her walls were covered with framed botanical drawings that on closer inspection he saw had been signed Emma Lawrence, Agnès's mother before she married Guy Prideaux.

He'd never told her he'd been in the house, been in her room.

Like the greenhouse, it was private. Her place. You had to wait to be invited in. He'd broken the rules and, for the only time in his life, wished he hadn't.

Suzanna cleared her throat. 'Do you have everything you need, Mr Faulkner? Is your room comfortable?'

He thought about it. 'Maybe another pillow?' he suggested.

'Of course. I'll see to it.'

He was grinning as he took the stairs two at

a time. Obviously Agnès had warned her that he might not be staying.

She was wrong about that.

He was back for good.

He changed into jeans and trainers, took a pair of boots and a small backpack from the boot of his car and headed down the path to the creek.

Agnès took the case containing the pearl and diamond parure from the safety deposit box in the London security vault.

It had been a gift to Lady Anne from Sir Gerard Prideaux on the first day of their honeymoon. There was a portrait of her by Romney in the hall at the castle. It needed cleaning but her radiance still shone through two centuries of woodsmoke from the fireplace.

Beside her bed, there was a silver-framed copy of the photograph that had appeared in *Devon Life* of her parents on their wedding day. Her mother had been wearing the earrings, and the tiara was holding her veil in place.

She reached out and touched one of the earrings, her throat tight as she remembered that last moment, the rustle of silk, the elusive scent as her mother bent to kiss her goodnight before she and her father had driven off to a reception for the Lord Lieutenant of the County. There were pictures of that night in the county magazine, too. Men in dinner jackets, women in expensive gowns, their best jewellery on display. Her parents laughing at something.

She could still hear the dull thud of the knock waking her.

She had climbed out of bed to see police at the door. Not some poor constable faced with the terrible task of delivering bad news, but the assistant commissioner in his silver trimmed uniform, with a family support officer at his side. Her job, no doubt, had been to make the tea.

The parure was the only thing of any great worth Agnès personally owned and was infinitely precious.

This was her last resort.

She'd hung on until the very last moment, hoping against hope for some sort of miracle, but Kam's arrival had brought home the reality of her situation. How close she was to disaster.

It wasn't just her and her grandmother she had to care for. She had a duty to the people who worked at the castle, who lived there, had looked to her to keep things going.

This pretty trifle would pay for a new boiler, repair the roof, employ a professional to build the kind of website a modern events destination demanded. Selling it meant burning her boats.

It wasn't the jewels themselves. That life was gone. There would be no big wedding for her with photographs in all the society magazines.

This had been her exit plan and if the business failed there would be nothing to fall back on.

She took one last look then closed the case and placed it carefully in her tote bag.

No one else was going to lose their home on her watch.

CHAPTER FOUR

It's done. I dropped off Mama's parure at the auction house and then went to sit in St James's Park for a while before I caught the train home. Their jewellery expert was not available, but they are going to phone with an estimate of value early next week.
Agnès Prideaux's Journal

'WHATEVER TIME DID you start this morning?' Suzanna asked, when she put her head around her office door and saw the scatter of sticky notes Agnès had been scribbling, stuck in colour-coded rows on her whiteboard.

'I had some ideas I wanted to get down on paper. Did Kam Faulkner leave yesterday afternoon?'

'No, but he wanted to know when you'd be back.'

'You told him I'd gone to London?'

'I didn't tell him anything, Agnès. He already knew you'd gone out but I'm a bit concerned about him.'

'Concerned?'

'He said he was going to take the dinghy and go across to the island. I explained about the storm damage, that it was off-limits to guests—'

'But he went anyway. Kam never believed that the words "off-limits" applied to him. Don't worry about it, Suzanna. He knows the creek and the island better than anyone.'

'But that's what I'm trying to tell you. When Pam went to make up his room this morning his bed hadn't been slept in.' She gave an awkward little shrug. 'I did wonder...'

'If we'd made up when I came back?' She smiled. 'Sorry, Suz, it wasn't that kind of row. It's business.'

'Oh.' She looked disappointed. 'I could have sworn there was some sort of vibe between the two of you.'

'Ancient history,' Agnès said, dismissing it as if it were no more than a teen crush. 'He'll be back in his own good time. Is that for me?'

Suzanna looked down at the package she was holding. 'Oh, no. That's why I was looking for Mr Faulkner. This came for him by courier. It's marked urgent.'

On a Sunday?

Agnès took it and turned it over. It was a thick envelope, but it was enclosed in a plastic courier envelope and there was no way of knowing who it was from.

'Have you tried calling his phone?'

'It went straight to voicemail.'

'Okay,' she said, standing up and stretching out her back, her neck.

With the prospect of a serious amount of hard cash to play with she'd been lying awake, her mind running on how best to use it. The boiler had to be first, repairs to the roof and gutters; the rest she would have to use wisely to create a viable business. In the end she'd given up on sleep and had been in her office since long before dawn, playing with ideas.

'Leave it with me, Suz. I could do with some fresh air. And coffee.'

'You're going over there?' Suzanna followed her to the kitchen. 'On your own?'

She filled her coffee mug, took a sip, grinned. 'Are you volunteering to come with me?' she asked, well aware of Suz's aversion to small boats.

'Er…'

'I have my phone,' she said, taking pity on her. 'If I find Kam's bleeding body, I'll dial 999.'

She looked shocked. 'You don't think—?'

'I'm kidding, Suz.'

'Oh.' Then, 'You seem a bit chirpier this morning.'

'Chirpy might be pushing it,' she said, filling a second plastic mug and tightening the lid. She wrapped up a couple of croissants left over from breakfast and put everything in her bag. 'If I'm not back by four, call the coastguard.'

Kam heard the engine before it rounded the island and Agnès brought the small vessel expertly alongside the dock.

'You're disturbing the fish,' he said as she slung a rope around an upright to prevent it drifting off.

'Have you got a licence for that?' she replied,

nodding in the direction of the line extending from a rod propped against a tree where it was screened from the creek.

'What do you think?'

She hesitated, unsure. He hid a smile. Off balance she would be easier to deal with.

'I think you're being a nuisance. Suz was worried I'd find you with a broken ankle or worse.'

'So you came sailing to my rescue in that noisy little wasp?'

'I tried to rescue you once before,' she said, 'but my grandfather wouldn't listen to me.'

'I'm sure he had plenty to say.'

She just looked around at the bivouac he'd made with the dinghy's tarpaulin, the deep hollow he'd dug for his fire so that the glow wouldn't be spotted by anyone passing by.

'Old habits die hard,' she said, a fact borne out by the remains of the sea trout he'd caught and cooked for his supper, eaten cold for his breakfast.

'Did he hurt you?'

'No.' She shook her head. 'He didn't say or do

anything.' And yet her knuckles as she clutched at her bag were white. 'Did he hurt you?'

'No.' She didn't look convinced—they both knew that her grandfather had a violent temper—but it was the truth. 'Maybe it was the shock.'

'Maybe.' The absurdity of the idea provoked a wry smile. 'I'm sorry about yesterday, Kam. I want to explain.'

'There's nothing like a bacon sandwich to improve my hearing.'

'No bacon, I'm afraid, but I have hot coffee and an almond croissant. Take it or leave it.'

'I'll take it,' he said, shifting along the log to make room for her.

After the barest hesitation, just long enough to show that she wasn't going to be a pushover, she sat beside him, opened her bag and handed over a reusable mug and a pastry.

They sat in silence for a while, eating, drinking their coffee, listening to the clang of rigging on the yachts moored in the marina, the cries of gulls. Watching the wash of the creek as it flowed around the island.

'Some of the best memories are of moments I spent here,' he said, after a while.

'And the worst.'

'The past is another country, Agnès.'

'Foreign,' she said, correcting him. 'It's "The past is a foreign country; they do things differently there."' He raised an eyebrow. 'It's from a book. *The Go-Between.* You picked it up one day, when we were in the greenhouse, read the first few lines and then dismissed it as girls' stuff.'

'That sounds like me.'

She shook out the last dregs of her coffee, replaced the lid and put the mug back in her bag. 'I'm sorry about the state of your cottage, Kam. That you had to see it like that. I tried to persuade Grandfather to let me renovate it so that we could use it for a holiday let, but he never listened to women.'

'And after he died there was no money.'

She sighed. 'It's on my five-year plan.'

'I don't think it can wait that long.'

'No.' She glanced at him. 'How did you get in?'

'I don't imagine any of the windows would

have offered much of a challenge but, when we left, I put my key under a stone. A promise that I'd be back.'

'And here you are.'

'Everything I've done since that day has brought me one step nearer to making Priddy Castle my home.'

'The castle. That was a big ambition.'

'And yet, as you say, here I am. I'm just sorry your grandfather is not alive for me to spit in his eye while I take it from him.'

She grasped the log and looked up into the sky. Either the sun was making her eyes water or that was a tear running from the corner of her eye.

'Tell me about the entail,' he said, resisting the urge to reach out and hold her, comfort her. 'Shouldn't the estate have gone to the next male in line? Isn't that how it worked back in the bad old days?'

She gave a little sniff, but her voice was steady enough as she said, 'The entail simply states that the estate can only be inherited by someone born in the castle. There is no distinction between male and female. If, for any reason, the family can't hold it, then it automatically passes to Henri Prideaux's descendants through his first wife.'

Clearly there was a story there, but he was more interested in the present. 'Is it possible for an entail to be broken?'

'If all the relevant parties agree,' she said.

'Are you saying that Henri's French descendants are still out there?'

'He wasn't French. Henri was from the island of Norhou, off the coast of Brittany.'

'I've never heard of it.'

'Back then it was a rats' nest of smugglers. Nationality meant nothing to them and they spoke their own patois. During the Napoleonic wars there were important people on both sides of the Channel who used it to make a fortune in illicit trade. Notionally it's part of France but is governed by a *seigneur*, a title held by Henri. Having inherited it, his son arrived with an armed force to claim the castle but Elizabeth rang the bell in the tower to summon the local militia.'

Kam smiled to himself. Was that where

Agnès had inherited her resolve? Her determination?

'He didn't return?'

'No, but an emissary from Norhou has never failed to arrive at the castle, on the death of the incumbent Prideaux, to check the resolve of the new heir. One went so far as to propose marriage to the widow over her husband's coffin.'

'And when your grandfather died?'

'Pierre Prideaux, the present Seigneur of Norhou, presented himself at Grandfather's funeral.'

There was an edge to her voice.

Until that moment this had all been a story, ancient history, but this was different. This was about Agnès and that made it personal… 'Did he make you the same offer?'

'Nothing so attractive,' she said, refusing to meet his gaze.

'What could have been worse? I'd like to know what I'm up against,' he said, when she shook her head.

'You're thinking of making me a counter offer? Save your breath, Kam, you don't have a horse in this race.' He waited and finally she threw up a hand. 'If you must know he's fifty if he's a day, has two ex-wives and a mistress he was quick to inform me that he had no intention of giving up.'

She had turned away and didn't see his instinctive urge to reach out to her, hold her. Relieved, he let his arm drop, unnoticed.

'Where were you expected to fit in in this ménage?' he asked, as if it were no more than casual interest.

'I was to be available when he visited the castle, although he had no objection to me taking a lover during his absence if I was discreet. He'd taken steps to ensure that he had no more children so if I thought to cheat him by becoming pregnant, I would lose everything.'

'I imagine he thought he was doing you a favour,' he said, to disguise an outrage that he had no business feeling. He'd been feeling far too much since he'd watched Agnès having that disastrous telephone conversation with the plumber and it wasn't the anger that had been driving him for as long as he could remember. 'It would have given you everything you want.'

The look she gave him should have turned him to stone.

'He was lucky I didn't throw him and his oily tongue in the creek.'

Not 'have him thrown' but 'throw him', Kam noticed, doing his best not to smile at her fierceness. And not succeeding.

'What's so funny?' she demanded.

'Nothing. I was just remembering cheering you when you caught your first fish and you called me a patronising oaf.'

'You didn't know what it meant.'

'I looked it up in the dictionary when I got home. It was pretty cutting from a six-year-old.'

'I was a precocious brat,' she said, 'and you were mean and wouldn't let me use your rod after that. I had to go up into the spidery attic to find my own.'

For a moment they were both grinning at the memory but then, as if remembering why he'd come, she looked away and he said, 'Prideaux must want the estate very badly.'

'I could smell the hunger on him and I'm not the only one under financial pressure. Pierre lost a lot of money during the banking crisis.'

'How would the castle help? It's loaded with debt.'

'The entail ends once it is passed to that side of the family. Unlike me, he would be free to sell off the choicest bits of the estate to developers.'

'Developers?' That would mean this untouched side of the creek would be carved up into plots for holiday homes occupied for just a few weeks a year. 'Do you know what he has in mind?'

'He didn't confide in me, but I was informed that he and another man thoroughly explored the estate while he was here. I was also told that, coincidentally, a surveyor from London was staying locally.'

'Where exactly?' he asked.

She glanced at him. 'The Ferryside Inn. Does it matter?'

He curbed the urgency in his voice. 'I meant what part of the creek?'

'Oh, I see. Is that why you're here? Is that how you've made the money to buy such an extravagant car, stay in the Captain's Suite?'

'Good grief, Agnès, nothing could be further

from the truth. I founded an online textile business that went public a couple of months ago.'

'Textiles?'

'Clothing, bedding, curtains…'

She stared at him. 'There was a story on the news recently about a company that started out on a market stall. They were talking about hundreds of millions.'

He lifted a shoulder, almost embarrassed at the amount of money involved. 'Now you know. So can we talk business?'

She shook her head. 'It makes no difference, Kam. I can't sell. Of course, if you were looking for an investment opportunity?' she prompted, only half seriously.

'An investment? What would I get out of it? You're never going to make a profit.' He'd been more abrupt than he'd intended. 'I want to own the land I walk on, Agnès. Own any roof over my head that I call home.'

'So why here? Why not buy yourself an island in the Caribbean, or somewhere fabulous in France or Italy with a vineyard and a swimming pool?'

'Because when I think of home, this is the place in my head. In my heart,' he added.

He hadn't realised that, but sitting here with Agnès on their log brought home to him how deep his feelings went, not just for this place, but for her.

She, on the other hand, was staring at him as if he'd grown two heads. Large sums of money had that effect on people, he'd discovered.

'You were going to tell me where the surveyor went,' he reminded her.

'Yes…' She shook her head as if to clear it. 'I was told they used a boat to travel along the entire creek frontage but were most interested in the section from the footpath that comes down through the woods to the far side of the beach.'

'The beach?'

Her throat moved as she swallowed and there was a faint flush on her cheek.

Was she thinking about that last night he'd camped on the island? The night she'd left her clothes on the beach and swum across in the moonlight…

He'd never forget the sight of her emerging from the creek, water running from her naked body as she'd walked up the tiny beach beside the dock to stand in a shaft of moonlight. Young, innocent, desperate…

'Show me,' he said, his voice thicker as it squeezed through his throat. 'Show me exactly where they were.'

'What's the point?'

The point was that he had to know what he was dealing with, what he was fighting and, without thinking, he offered her his hand as he stood up.

She raised her eyebrows. 'Do I look decrepit?'

'You look tired and stressed out.' And lovely, he thought, in way that the unlived-in face of a teenage girl could never be. 'Also, your chef warned me to treat you like a lady,' he said. 'I got the impression that if you appeared with so much as a scratch he'd serve up my liver in onion gravy as a lunchtime special.'

That finally provoked a laugh. 'Jamie is a sweetie.'

'Not a patronising oaf?'

A faint flush stained her cheeks. 'I'm not six,' she said. 'Or sixteen.'

'I've noticed.'

The flush deepened.

'Jamie is a trained chef,' she said. 'He hates the menu he is forced to serve in the Orangery just as much as I do. It makes him a touch grouchy.'

'If that's his problem,' he said, 'why does he stay?'

'Why do you think? He needs a job.'

If he was a trained chef, he could get a job anywhere. Did she not realise that the man was in love with her?

'Come on, then, Sir Galahad,' she said, grasping his hand as she stood up. The moment her fingers touched his, a tingle of electricity rippled up his arm and he had to step back to regain his balance and she was the one supporting him. She shook her head. 'You're going to have to do better than that if you're going to be my knight errant.' And when he didn't move, 'Get a move on, Kam. I'm sure you know this island better than I do. And if there are any stray roots intent on tripping up interlopers, I'd rather it was you who fell on your face.'

As her hand slipped from his, he found himself clutching the space where it had been and had to curl his fingers into a fist before he made a fool of himself.

It was, apparently, only him being turned over by old memories.

A few minutes later, having fought his way through the overgrown footpath, holding back who knew how many years of dry, vicious brambles so that she wouldn't be scratched, they were looking across at the beach.

Hidden from the creek by the island, this was where the smugglers had unloaded their cargo, carrying it into a cave and through a tunnel into the cellars under the tower.

There were wooden steps leading up from the beach to a grassy meadow topping a low bluff.

'Here?' He surveyed the meadow. Away from the woods, it was lighter, warmer. There were already bluebells among the red and white campion and, later, there would be fritillaries and wild orchids.

'He's planning to rip up this meadow?'

'I don't know what he's planning, but I suggest you sit down and enjoy it while you can.'

Agnès curled up on the grass, her feet tucked

under her, and patted the ground beside her as if he were a child about to be taught a lesson.

Who was patronising who now?

There was definitely a change in her manner, a new confidence that disturbed him. He wanted to know what had changed, but even more he wanted to discover the scent of the woman she'd become, watch the way her hair slid over her shoulder, reacquaint himself with her profile…

'I'd forgotten how peaceful it is on the island,' she said. 'You can't see the castle from here. You can't see the creek, hear anything but the birds. You could be lost in the wilderness.'

'Why don't you take a photograph from here for your website? A wildflower walk would draw the visitors and you would make a great guide.'

She turned to look at him. 'That is actually a great idea.'

'Don't sound so surprised,' he said, as she took out her phone and started taking some shots.

She laughed. 'Sorry, Mr Multimillionaire.

Obviously you are overflowing with great ideas.'

'Okay, then, here's another. Make it into a picnic. Are you allowed to cater on the estate, or is it all tied up in that contract? Is the castle kitchen certified to serve food to the public?'

'Yes, but it's not large enough for mass catering. We do breakfast for the B & B guests and supper for the craft groups and I think, if I made it a garden package, I could do it. I'll have to check but I have to get lucky once in a while.'

'It doesn't work that way.'

'No.' The smile faded. 'I'd like to live here with this view. One day, if the castle becomes so successful that I need more rooms, I shall build a little cabin tucked away back there in the trees and make it my home.'

About to say that the castle was her home, he remembered her childhood bedroom with its lack of comfort.

She'd still been in the nursery when her parents were killed by a drunk driver.

Clearly, when she'd grown out of that, her grandparents hadn't cared enough to make her room special in any way. The only personal touch had been her mother's botanical drawings that had been hung on the walls.

His childhood had not been easy after his father left; there had been no money. But there had been love in abundance.

'You seem more optimistic about the future today,' he said.

'Do I?'

She didn't seem inclined to offer an explanation and he didn't push it.

Sitting beside her, he had gradually become aware of a light, citrusy scent above the salty tang of the creek. Had she been in the Orangery this morning, checking on her orange trees? Having a moment with the sweet, protective chef?

Did her dreams of the island cabin include him?

Kam knew he shouldn't care but then, as she glanced at him, apparently seeking some kind of response to her wishful thinking, the breeze caught a loose strand of her silky dark hair, whipping it across her face. Without taking her eyes off him, she reached up with both arms, one to recapture the strand, the other to fasten it into place with the silver clasp that was holding it back from her face.

The gesture seemed deliberately erotic, like a painting by Manet he'd once seen in Paris, men in suits with naked women having a picnic in the woods, and for a moment his only thought was to lie back in the grass, taking her down with him.

Not as some unfulfilled boyhood fantasy. This wasn't the young naked Agnès who had lived in his memory like a thorn burning in his flesh. This was a new, unexpected, unlooked-for response to the woman she had become, the desire so immediate, so shockingly intense that it was as if the breath had been knocked from him.

His face must have telegraphed his thoughts because that moment of perfect poise disintegrated into confusion as she fumbled the clasp and her hair cascaded around her face.

The invitation had been all in his mind. Of course it had. He had been aggressive, rude even. Why would she give him a second thought when she had sweet Jamie?

She was gathering up her hair now, looking anywhere but at him. Watching her made him feel like a voyeur and he turned away.

He hadn't come to Priddy Castle to rekindle an adolescent romance, he reminded himself. Far from it. He hadn't expected to feel anything but satisfaction at seeing her on the brink of losing everything.

Which made him an idiot.

You never forgot your first love. Not one that had grown organically over the best part of ten years until you could read each other's minds, finish each other's sentences.

When they'd been together she would pass him a tool, or a net, or a line before he knew he wanted it. She'd always had a smile but he'd always known when it was a mask and saved new things to show her on those days, new stuff to teach her.

And when he'd told her that he wanted to learn to play the guitar, she'd smuggled an old and very beautiful acoustic instrument out of the castle and given it to him, asking only that one day, when he had learned to play, that he play a song just for her.

He still owed her that song. Maybe it was as well that the guitar was in his London apartment because he'd never forget the moment when, with a look, everything changed. When instead of taking her to see badger cubs, he wanted to take her to his school prom and show everyone that she was his girl.

When instead of showing off the way the osprey he'd rescued flew to his whistle for a fish, he'd wanted to find the perfect song, the one that said everything he was feeling, and sing it to her.

He'd buried all those feelings under layers of rage that he'd wrapped around him, clinging on as tightly as an infant clung to a comfort blanket. He'd had to, because if he couldn't blame her for what had happened, then he would have had to blame himself.

He'd understood the risk. He'd known he should have brought some girl from town to the estate, making out that he was all over her so that Agnès would have believed that he was not interested.

He hadn't been able to do it and instead he'd just confused her by keeping his distance.

She hadn't been the girl to let him get away with that.

'Is your optimism well founded?' he asked, when she'd stopped fiddling with her hair.

'It's too early to say but…' She paused, glanced across at him, waiting for a prompt.

'But?' he obliged.

'If I could pay off enough of the tax bill to hold off bankruptcy, I could offer a hotel chain a long-term lease to develop this site.'

What? 'You're not serious?'

She looked deadly serious.

'Why not? If it's going to happen anyway.' She sketched a shrug. 'The wildflower walks are a lovely idea and I'll certainly use it for this year, but I'm going to need more than a few picnics to repair the roof.'

'Can you even do that? Sell a lease?'

'My great-great-grandfather sold ninety-nine-year repairing leases on the properties down on the quay. He didn't want the upkeep to be a burden on the estate—tenants insisting on proper plumbing, bathrooms, roofs that didn't leak, all that tedious twentieth-century stuff. It must have seemed like a sensible plan at the time. These days they would make a substantial rental income. More than enough to keep the castle in good shape.'

'So why haven't you already done it?' he asked. 'Why didn't your grandfather?'

'The quayside properties were built on land that wasn't part of the original estate plan. I'm going to need a fancy lawyer to make the case for a precedent and they cost money.'

'I'm sure a developer would be prepared to pay for the legal work if he thought there was a chance of getting his hands on that, but I thought you loved this place as much as I do. Would you really sell your birthright…?'

'For a mess of pottage?' She finished the question for him when he realised he'd been reduced to quoting from the bible and decided to stop making an ass of himself. 'Needs must, Kam. And just look at it.'

As she made a sweeping gesture that took in the scene before them, the sun flashed on something metallic and he realised that she was wearing the bangle with a little fish charm that he'd bought her for her fifteenth birthday.

Was it an accident? Had she just picked it up

and slipped it on this morning without thinking about where it had come from? Had she forgotten that he'd given it to her?

He'd seen it in an antique shop window and it had cost him two days' dodging the river wardens while he caught enough sea trout to pay for it. But he'd known, the minute he'd set eyes on it, that she would love it.

CHAPTER FIVE

Spending time on the island with Kam, teasing him a little, was fun. I hoped he'd notice that I was wearing the bracelet he gave me but he didn't say anything. Maybe he doesn't remember.

Agnès Prideaux's Journal

'LOOK, KAM...'

'I am looking,' he said.

'It's got everything. Creek frontage, a private beach, space—'

'I'm not a property developer. You don't have to sell it to me.'

'—space for a small marina,' she continued as if he hadn't spoken. 'All it needs is a pretty bridge.'

'A bridge?'

'To the island. Can't you see it? With the debris, the brambles cleared away, a pretty new summer house, flowering shrubs, it would be perfect for private parties and weddings. Of course, you couldn't ferry everyone back and forth by boat, especially when they'd a few too many glasses of champagne.'

He stared at her. Was she serious?

This was their island.

'That's appalling. Think of the habitat destruction. There's an eco system that has been here undisturbed for hundreds of years. And isn't the wildflower meadow an SSI? A site of scientific special interest.'

'It is,' she said, lifting her shoulders in regretful shrug. 'But think of the money.'

'Agnès …'

Too late he caught the gleam in her eye, a tiny movement at the corner of her mouth, as she glanced in his direction.

He'd remembered so clearly the moments when her face betrayed every emotion. How could he have forgotten the way she could keep a straight face while leading him on with some nonsense?

She raised a *Got you* eyebrow and he conceded with a shake of the head as she laughed. 'If you could see your face.'

'It's not funny.'

'No,' she admitted. 'But that's what will happen if I lose it.'

'Really? Surely there would be an outcry at the vandalism. It would take years to get planning consent.'

'I'd like to think so but the recession has been hard on the town and a resort hotel would bring in much-needed business. People with money to spend. New jobs.'

'Mammon cancels out the environment? The locals might not care but I'm sure I could whip up a storm of protest on social media. Pierre Prideaux sounds like a pragmatist. You can't sell to me, but once HMRC declares you bankrupt I'll offer him my deal. Money in the bank against a fight all the way to the Secretary of State for the Environment.'

'*If*,' she stressed, 'not when. If things go that far he won't need you or your money. Pierre's had over a year since my grandfather died to prepare for this. I imagine he took the surveyor's report along with detailed plans of what could be achieved here to the money men in Paris or Frankfurt or even London. It would be a major investment opportunity and I have no doubt he has all the deals in place just waiting for his moment. You won't have a chance to make your pitch, Kam. The money will change hands the moment he has control.'

She hadn't been teasing him, he realised. She had been giving him a glimpse of the future.

A unique stretch of the creek was going to be destroyed and there was nothing he could do to stop it. Only she could do that and it was why, against all the odds, she was fighting a David and Goliath battle with nothing but steely determination.

She'd made mistakes but she hadn't given up and he admired her for that, but if she fought to the bitter end, sold what personal assets remained, she'd be left with nothing.

'Is there anything we can do to stop it?' he asked.

'We?'

She acknowledged the shared goal with a half-smile, reached out and briefly touched his hand. 'It'll be fine,' she said. 'I have a plan.'

'It's going to take more than selling the family silver,' he warned. 'If you have something valuable to sell, a way out, my advice would be to save what you can and walk away.'

'Cut and run, Kam? Is that what you'd do?'

What he would do had no bearing on this. 'I'm warning you not to throw good money after bad. You used to listen to me.'

'Not always.'

'No,' he acknowledged. He'd told her that he didn't have time for her that summer, gone to the island to keep out of her way, but she'd come anyway.

For a moment she held his gaze, then sighed. 'You mean well, Kam. You obviously know what you're talking about. Unfortunately, this isn't just about me, it's about all the people who work on the estate. I thought you, more than anyone, would understand that.'

'Why?' he asked, pushing her now, wanting her to face reality. 'Do you really believe that when the chips are down they will care about you? Will thank you for your sacrifice?'

She looked stricken. 'I know you think that no one cared about you, Kam, but it's not true.

My grandfather wouldn't talk to me but there were people who worked here who tried to get him to change his mind.'

'Your grandmother?' he asked. 'She and my mother were friends. I understood why I was going to be banished, but my mother had done nothing.'

'Grandma…' She swallowed, shook her head. 'I begged her to intervene, but she said it was a waste of breath. She told me that he'd been looking for an excuse to get rid of your mother for months, that I'd given it to him and I'd have to live with it on my conscience.'

'Is that supposed to make me feel better?'

'No, it's supposed to make you want to *do* better. Or are you just like Pierre Prideaux? Do you just want to be king of the castle?'

'Would you blame me?'

He felt a cold hand squeeze his heart as the words slipped from his mouth. Was that, deep down, all he wanted? Were his grand plans just an excuse? Was he really that shallow?

'Tell me who you care about,' he said, before she could answer.

Would it be the chef who hated what he did

but needed the job? His stomach tightened at the thought. Which was stupid. She was only a year, eighteen months, younger than him.

There were no twenty-six-year-old virgins and even in his darkest days he wouldn't have wished that barren a life on her. And Jamie, rot his socks, obviously cared for her. Maybe they'd end up together running a little boutique restaurant down on the quay.

Not if he could help it…

The thought fell into his mind and lodged there.

Not if he could help it.

'Why would you care?' she demanded. 'You're like all men. You just want everyone to see how big you are.'

There was an element of truth in that. Maybe a bigger element than he'd care to admit. He'd sworn he'd come back to Castle Creek on top of the world and, against all the odds, he'd done it. But Agnès was right. This wasn't just about him. Caught up in the past, he was in danger of losing sight of the real reason he'd come back to Castle Creek.

'Give me a reason to care, Agnès,' he said

and, as uncertainty flickered in her wide, grey eyes, 'Make me care.'

Agnès took a moment. Letting the swish of the current, the scent of crushed spring grass, calm her as she tried to read Kam.

She'd slipped on the bracelet he'd given her this morning hoping that he'd remember a time when they had been friends. He hadn't noticed, or hadn't remembered, but even so there had been moments when they had seemed to come close to recapturing something of that time, maybe something more, something new. Then he'd say something outrageous and it was gone.

It had been fun to tease him a little, though, to know that she could still draw him in.

There was no way he could have the castle, but maybe, if they could forget the bad bits of the past and just remember the good, they might at least be friends. Maybe more than friends.

She glanced at him, He'd always been able to hide his feelings—she'd learned to deadpan from him. There was nothing coming back, nothing to give her a clue as to what he was thinking, feeling, but he'd challenged her to make him care.

'Well, there's Tim,' she said, at last.

He raised his eyebrows as if that was not the name he expected to hear.

'He works in the garden,' she explained.

'I've met Tim. He turfed me out of your greenhouse.'

'Did he?' Damn. There she was attempting to be the socially aware and caring adult but all it took was one word and she was twelve years old, curled up in her armchair with Kam on an old rug, his back against the wall. Winter sun was warming them through the glass, they had huge mugs of hot chocolate and sausages, fried on her little gas stove, that she'd stuffed into soft rolls…

'What on earth were you doing in the greenhouse?' she asked.

'What do you think? I was looking for you after you stormed off. You're still trying to breed new roses, I notice. How is that going?'

'It's a slow business and most aren't worth developing.'

'Most?'

'There are a couple that have been accepted by the RHS. There's a very sweet pink half double that the bees love that I named Emma Prideaux, for my mother.'

'And the other?'

'The other is cream with a pink blush called Jenny Faulkner,' she said. 'Your mother was always so kind to me.'

Kam looked as if she'd hit him with a brick. 'I don't know what to say.'

'I have one in a pot that you can give to her. If you think she would take it from me.'

'I…yes…but you must give it to her yourself.'

She felt a ridiculous glow of pleasure. And hope. 'I'd like that.'

He nodded, briefly, then said, 'Where did you go, Agnès? Yesterday.'

Okay. The brief interlude of reminiscence was over and it was back to business but she wasn't going to tell him yet. She had to know how much she was likely to get for the parure before she dared believe that she might save the castle. That, if she could make a go of it, she would have a child one day, even if she had to use a donor, so that there would be a new generation to hold the castle against all comers.

'Did you eat the lunch first?' she asked, quite deliberately changing the subject. 'Before you looked for me?'

He looked at her for a moment, clearly considering whether to push it, but then said, 'I didn't risk it. I had the feeling that Jamie would spit in it.'

She grinned. 'What did you say when he told you to treat me like a lady?'

'That I knew you before you were a lady.'

'Shockingly predictable, Kam.'

'But true.'

'While you were always the perfect gentleman. Not.'

'My mother was hot on good manners,' he protested.

'They weren't in evidence the first time I tagged along after you.'

'I told you to go home, but you were impossible to shake off no matter how rude I was.'

'You didn't try very hard once I offered you a bap stuffed with bacon and scrambled egg, which should have been my breakfast.'

'I wish I had it now.'

'You should have stayed and eaten your lunch. Jamie has too much pride in his work to do anything as gross as spit in your food. He's marshmallow under that tough exterior, but he had a tough start and has a bit of form so he needs the job.'

'Form?'

'He punched his boss when he molested a young waitress.'

'Did he? Damn. I was trying so hard not to like him.'

'Unfortunately he broke the man's jaw. He got a suspended sentence, so he needs to stay out of trouble and it's quiet here.'

'I think he stays for more than the quiet.'

She waited for him to elaborate but he said, 'Tell me about Tim.'

She frowned at his sudden sharpness. 'What do you want to know?'

'How did you find him?' he asked, rather more gently.

'He found me. His mother used to bring him to the garden at least once a week. Tim was fascinated by the plants, but particularly the roses and my attempt to breed new varieties. Since he was here anyway I asked him if he would like to help out in the garden for a few hours a week in return for a special pass to allow him and his mother to come any time they liked.'

'That's no way to build a business.'

'On the contrary, most stately homes and big gardens use volunteers to keep the weeds under control, the grass cut. When things are settled I'm going to start a Friends of Priddy Castle group. Come as often as you like for an annual fee, special events, a chance to see parts of the garden and castle not open to the public. An annual party. And of course take part in work parties.'

'You don't pay volunteers,' he pointed out, not to be distracted. 'Tim told me you pay him above the minimum wage.'

'You two did have a nice chat.'

'Yes, we did, before he escorted me out of a part of a garden where, apparently, I had no right to be.'

'He's very protective.'

'A trait you seem to engender in all the men you meet.'

'Not all,' she said. 'You led me into plenty of scrapes.'

'And saved you from a good many. You'd have drowned trying to swim across the creek if I hadn't been there to hold you up. You didn't even thank me.'

'It was you who dared me…!'

'I tried to stop you.'

'No…' But even as she said it a memory of him chasing after her flickered into life. 'Yes, you did. How could I have got that so wrong?'

'You knew you'd behaved like a spoiled brat and put us both at risk. It undoubtedly scared you witless so your brain edited the memory.'

'Yes… I'm so sorry. Thank you, Kam.'

'Any time,' he said, so softly that his voice was little more than a vibration in the air and for a moment neither of them moved, spoke.

'You were telling me about Tim,' he prompted after a while.

'Tim…' For a moment she'd been lost in the past, remembering precious moments, and she grabbed at something that was the present, tangible… 'He turned up every day as if he had a job and I had to pay him. I'd pay him more if I could afford it. He knows all the roses by name, treats each one as if it's a friend. And I love the way he reassures the grass when he's mowing it. *"Nothing to worry about. Just like me going for a haircut..."'* she said, in a fair approximation of Tim's voice.

Kam, who had been veering between friendly interest, irritable and an unexpected tenderness that made her want to weep, was now struggling to hide a smile.

'How does he cope with the kitchen garden?' he asked. 'Doesn't he object to digging up carrots, cutting cabbage?'

'Apparently vegetables are different. He still treats them with the greatest tenderness, gives them all his love while they're growing, but he said it's no different from cutting flowers for the house. They are fulfilling their role in the natural order of things.'

'So he's a treasure.'

'A treasure?'

'That's what your grandmother used to call my mother. Her treasure.'

And with that Kam's smile faded and her

guilt returned. Her wickedness had lost her grandmother her only friend and ally.

One of the cleaners told her that her grandfather had threatened Kam with the police for touching his underage granddaughter unless his mother left without a fuss.

It had only been a couple of weeks until her birthday, but she would have been back at school by then and it would have been Christmas before she'd see him again.

She had behaved like that spoilt brat who'd plunged into the creek wanting to show Kam that he was wrong.

Everyone had blamed her and no amount of brain editing would ever delete the memory of those last few days before she went back to school when no one would speak to her.

'Who else?' he asked, abruptly.

'What?'

'Who else should I care about?'

She forced herself to focus. 'Lily and Sandra. They're getting on a bit. Lily worked in the The Bread Oven in town, Sandra in that shop on the quay that sells buckets and spades. The Bread Oven was taken over by a chain that had a mandatory retirement age, and the owner of the bucket and spade shop had a daughter leaving school and in need of a job. They were both old enough to draw their pensions, sit back and put their feet up, but they were bored out of their minds within weeks. I met them when they came on a bluebell walk and we got talking.'

'The garden appears to be your recruiting agency.'

'It's a good place to get the measure of someone. They love the castle and, with the help of Pam and Savannah, they keep the place shining. Savannah was in foster care,' she added, quickly. 'When she left school, she had nowhere to go and her social worker asked me if I could take her on, give her a chance. She's starting a hospitality course at the local college in the autumn. And you've met Suz. Suzanna.'

'Your receptionist. Did you find her in the garden too?'

Where she'd found Suzanna was no one's business but their own.

'She's a lot more than a receptionist, she's a friend. She doesn't have any formal leisure industry qualifications but she's a born organiser and living in allows her to send money home to her family in Sudan.'

'So she's a refugee?'

'She has been given the right to remain in this country with me as her sponsor. I'm doing everything I can to get her ten-year-old sister here as a matter of urgency.'

'You are a one-woman social services agency. What about the staff in the Orangery? When you've been declared bankrupt, the official receiver will want a close look at their accounts.'

'You make it sound almost worth going under.'

'I don't buy your flippancy. Don't you care about them? What about your sweetie of a chef? He might lose his job.'

'I don't employ the Orangery staff.'

He raised an eyebrow at her. 'That's not in the caring, compassionate spirit you've been selling me.'

She shrugged. This was all speculation on Kam's part. It wasn't going to happen. She wasn't going to let it happen.

'I have no idea whether Pierre would want to keep the restaurant open, I am sure he'd rattle a lot better deal out of them before he'd let them stay than I managed, but the reality is that he would want French-speaking staff for the castle.'

'I thought you said he was going to sell the estate.'

'Only the stuff around the edges. The land down by the creek, and there's a field on the coastal side of the estate that someone wanted for a caravan park a few years back. He may keep Creek Cottage for staff, but he'll undoubtedly sell the freehold on the quayside properties to a property company.'

'That wouldn't be sensible. They can't have that long to run.'

'No, but Pierre doesn't care about the estate, or the people, or the creek. All he wants is what his ancestor Henri Prideaux wanted, Kam. What you can never be. To be Prideaux of Priddy Castle.'

Kam stared at her for one long moment then got to his feet and, without another word, headed back to his camp.

Agnès remained where she was, breathing in

the scent he left in the space where he had been. Woodsmoke, trampled grass, fresh salty air.

She felt bad about what she'd just said.

Kam has been totally upfront, not to say blunt, with her. He'd made his pile and the castle would be a statement to her, her grandmother and the town, that he had made it; moved on.

She was the one stuck in a life that had been written for her two hundred years ago. Stuck with the feelings he had churned up, feelings that she couldn't afford to indulge.

Agnès took out her phone and called Suz to reassure her that everything was well and that she'd be back shortly. Then she went after Kam, picking her way carefully past the brambles he'd protected her from when he'd led the way.

Kam must have heard her coming but he was fanning the embers of the fire and didn't look up.

'Will you be staying over here?' she asked.

'If it doesn't rain.'

'Since when did a drop of rain bother you? Don't tell me you're going soft.' He looked up briefly, his expression one of irritation that reminded her so much of the boy he'd been that she regretted not bringing a bacon bap with her. 'Is there anything you need?' she persisted.

'You can bring me a bacon bap in the morning,' he said, echoing her thoughts.

'Just bacon?'

He shrugged. 'You could add a dollop of scrambled egg. Maybe a couple of sausages.'

He was smiling now. 'You could fill that up, too,' he added, offering her the mug she'd filled with coffee for him. 'And I'll have another of those croissants.'

'You were a lot easier to please when you were a boy.'

'I'm not that boy, Agnès. I have a man's appetite.' The smile was replaced by an expression she had only seen once before, in that moment when she'd walked naked out of the creek.

She could still feel his rough fingers as he'd reached out and touched her breast before drawing her close… Still wanted him so badly that she could barely stand.

'Kam—'

'I'll have some freshly squeezed orange juice, too.'

She drew in a shaky breath, forced herself

to focus on this moment, this reality, deal with this and get away.

'We don't usually do take-outs…' Breathe, breathe… 'If you choose to sleep rough I can't stop you, but you'll still be charged for the suite, which means you're entitled to breakfast.'

She turned to go.

'Agnès.' She stopped but didn't turn back. 'I admire your loyalty to your staff, but your grandfather is to blame for your situation.'

She sighed. 'Grandma said once, when she'd had a few too many sherries, that when my parents were killed in that road accident, something in my grandfather broke. He stopped caring about the estate, saw no future in a girl child who ran wild in the woods. Who, when she finally grew up, refused to do her duty, parade herself in the marriage market and ensnare some unsuspecting chinless wonder with an inheritance.'

'Ensnare?'

'"*Get yourself up the duff, girl, like your mother…*" As if anyone thinks they have to marry these days.' She turned then to look at him. 'It wasn't true, about Mummy. I was a honeymoon baby, born nine months, three weeks and five days after the wedding, but he'd convinced himself that she'd trapped Daddy into marriage.' There were tears stinging at the backs of her eyes now, but she wouldn't cry. Mustn't cry…

But then Kam was holding her, his cheek rough against her temple, and nothing would stop the tears.

'He would have been so happy if she had been the only one to die in that crash,' she said, 'leaving my father free to marry someone more suitable. Someone with an inheritance to shore up the estate, someone who could have given him a proper—'

'Stop!' he said. 'Not another word.' And without knowing how it had happened he was kissing her just to stop her from saying the words. Then just because…

Agnès gave a little gasp and then, for one blissful moment, she was kissing him back, sweet and questioning before she had pulled back and was looking at him. For a moment anything might have happened, but then she said, 'Thank you,' before stepping back, leaving him with a big cold empty space in his arms.

Thank you…right…he took a breath, called his body back from the brink and said, 'Don't make excuses for him. Your grandfather was a bully and bigot and your grandmother was too weak to stand up to him.'

'I know.' She shivered as she acknowledged the truth. 'He wasn't broken, he was just outraged that a drunken nobody had been crass enough to wipe out his heir. Outraged that Grandma had failed to give him a spare. She was the one who was broken.' She shook her head. 'It doesn't matter. He's dead and I'm not asking for sympathy from you, Kam. Heaven knows I don't deserve it.'

She was shaking. So much for all that keep-calm-and-carry-on act, the teasing, those moments when she had thought that anything might happen. Anything just had, but it was just the place, the emotional fallout of the moment; as appealing as it might be, she didn't have time to indulge in a little catch-up affair with Kam. She was on her own and had to remain focussed or she would lose everything.

She lifted her head, took a step back, aware of his hand still overstretched to steady her.

'I've made arrangements…' Something caught in her throat and she was forced to stop but he waited and after a moment she said, 'In a few weeks I should have enough money to turn things around.'

'Agnès…'

He clearly thought she was delusional. Maybe she was, but if she failed…

'If I fail, if I can't hold on, if I can't stop Pierre Prideaux from taking the estate, selling it off in building lots to fill his coffers, I will burn the castle down, every stick and stone of it,' she said, 'before I'd let him spend one night in the home his ancestor stole two hundred years ago.'

For a long moment there was silence. Even the birds seemed to have stopped whatever they were doing to listen, open-beaked, to her passionate outburst.

Kam's hand was on Agnès's arm. She was shaking, or maybe it was him.

Then, gradually the world began to turn again. There was a clank as the ferry arrived at the quay, a gull shrieked over a fishing boat. Somewhere, far overhead, a blackbird began to sing.

He drew a breath, said, as gently as he knew how, 'You can't do that, Agnès.'

'I've shocked you.' Not a question, but a statement. 'Not for the first time.'

'No.' But this was very different from her Aphrodite act. This was fury at what was happening, of losing control, losing her home. He understood that. He'd made his own vow to an unfair universe, clung stubbornly to thoughts of revenge.

He was not proud of that, but his return wasn't about tearing the world down around him. It was about building something new. And Agnès, if she would let him in, could be a part of that.

She'd been stubborn as a child, following him with a determination that he hadn't been able to shake no matter how hard he'd made it for her. In that moment he saw that small girl, chin stuck out, as she'd huffed and puffed to keep up with him, and he had to know what was driving her.

'Will you tell me why you feel so strongly?'

She shook off his hand, took a step back. 'You're a man. You'd never understand.'

'I understand that you dislike him, that he made you a slimy proposition, that given the chance he will carve up an estate that has endured for centuries for a quick profit, but what is it about the castle? How did Henri steal it?'

For a moment she appeared to consider, but then she stiffened her back. 'That's family business.'

There was a look, a warning not to push it, but he couldn't leave it. There was something going on here that he didn't understand. Something he needed to get to the bottom of before she did something stupid and ended up in jail.

'You'll need someone to speak for you when you're in the dock for arson,' he pointed out.

'You'd do that for me?'

Right at that moment he would have done anything for her, but he needed to know why she felt so strongly. 'Will you tell me?'

She gave a little shake of her head. 'If it should come to that, I'll speak for myself.'

She didn't wait for a response but turned and

walked to the dock where the small speedboat was tied up and stepped aboard.

He didn't try to stop her or follow her, but he called after her. 'I don't want to develop the estate, Agnès. I won't construct a hotel complex on your meadow. I won't build expensive houses along the creek that the locals can't afford. I won't lease the coast field for a caravan park.'

'I know. Pierre will already have it all sewn up.'

He didn't bother to argue, just wished that he'd held her tighter, kissed her longer, done anything to stop her walking away from him.

She kept doing that but, sooner or later, driven by necessity, she would walk back and then, maybe, they could find a way back to something precious that had been taken from them, and then move forward to make a future here at the castle.

After two or three desperate attempts, she managed to start the outboard, startling the birds into flight.

When it was his, he would ban the use of outboards at the estate. Except that Agnès said she had accessed some money. Enough to keep going.

She had to be selling something. Not the family silver. What was left of it after her grandfather had sold the finest pieces wouldn't make the kind of money she needed.

It had to be something personal and the way she'd choked up meant that it was precious to her, presumably something left to her by one or other of her parents. Wills were a matter of public record, so it shouldn't be difficult to find out what it was.

He turned on his phone and called someone who, if he couldn't access it online, would have the information as soon as the probate office opened on Monday. Then he flipped through his messages until he found the one he was waiting for and smiled at the attached photograph.

He put out the fire, cleaned up his camp, took in his rod and stowed everything neatly away beneath the tarpaulin, which he covered with some of the fallen branches that littered the island. Then he stepped into the dinghy and rowed, without disturbing a single living thing, across the creek to the town, where he tied up at the quay.

CHAPTER SIX

Well, that didn't go exactly to plan. I intended to have a quiet chat with Kam on the privacy of the island, explain the situation in a calm and sensible manner, but calm flies out of the window when he's around. Arguing with him makes me feel alive. Kissing him makes me feel alive. Unfortunately he now thinks I'm a crazy arsonist.

Agnès Prideaux's Journal

AGNÈS TOOK HER grandmother a cup of tea, planning to stay for a while to give Pam a break. 'How are you feeling, Grandma?'

Her grandmother had dropped off to sleep in front of daytime television, but stirred, looked up and there was that moment of blankness Agnès dreaded before she said, 'You're very untidy, Agnès.'

She sighed with relief; today wasn't one of those days.

'You look as if you've been dragged through a hedge backwards. Whatever have you been doing?'

'It's a bit breezy out.' She sat down. 'Grandma, I need to tell you something.'

She wasn't listening, she was looking at the tray. 'You haven't brought me the biscuits I like.'

'I'm sorry. The guests finished them all.'

'Guests? What guests?' She'd forgotten the question the minute she'd asked it. 'I don't like these.' She picked them up and threw them across the room. Dora galloped after them. 'What did I tell you? They're dog biscuits.'

'Grandma,' she said, to get her attention. 'I need you to listen to me.'

'Why? You never make any sense.'

'It's important.'

She made an impatient gesture. 'Well, get on with it.'

'Do you remember Kam Faulkner?'

'Who?'

'Jenny Faulkner's son.'

'Jenny?' For a moment she looked blank and then her face lit up. 'Jenny was my treasure. She always brought me my favourite biscuits. Such a pretty woman. Hugo liked her a lot.'

'Did he?' Agnès frowned. 'You told me that he was desperate for an excuse to get rid of her.'

'Well, she didn't like him, did she? Wouldn't be nice to him and you know your grandfather, he always has to have his own way. She'd better stay out of his way.'

Nice?

'She isn't here, Grandma, just Kam. And Grandfather died last year.'

'You didn't bring the biscuits I like,' she grumbled. 'And for goodness' sake do something with your hair. You look a mess. You always did look a mess. Chasing after that boy like a little tramp. A lady wears it up,' she said. 'Where's Pam?'

'Having a break. I'll wait until she comes back.'

'You'll do as you're told for once and fix your hair.'

Dora, having eaten the biscuits, followed her in the hope of more and Agnès picked her up, tucking her under her arm, holding the warm little body close for a moment.

Dora wagged her tail, licked her hand as if she understood.

'I wasn't a tramp,' she whispered into her honey-coloured coat. 'I loved him. I still love him.' There had never been anyone else.

Pam, who had started working in the castle as a chambermaid before gradually become her grandmother's carer, was in the kitchen having a cup of tea. 'I'm sorry, Pam, she sent me away.'

'Your hair?' she asked.

It had been a battle since she'd turned eighteen. Wearing it loose, or clipped back, had been an act of defiance that she should have outgrown. 'Maybe I should just wear it up.'

Pam patted her arm. 'You wear it how you like, dear. If it wasn't that, it would be something else.'

'Biscuits. We've run out of those iced ones she likes.'

'I've got a pack in my bag.'

'You are my treasure, Pam. I don't know what I'd do without you.'

She used the mirror in her office to brush out

her hair and pin it up like the lady she would never be and tried not to think about what her grandmother had said.

There was no doubt about what 'nice' implied and she was horrified that Kam's lovely mother had been subjected to sexual harassment. Her grandfather couldn't have sacked her for not giving him what he wanted; she would have been able to take him to an employment tribunal and he'd have had to pay to shut her up.

He had just waited, sure that her teenage son would, sooner or later, give him just cause. Did Kam know? Had his mother told him?

'Forget it,' she told her reflection. 'No good will come of raking it up now.'

She had to focus on her plans for the future. Except that her mind was more interested in how she'd missed the fact that Kam had become a multimillionaire. A man with the kind of money to buy the estate, put it to rights and then pay staff, property taxes, the day-to-day running costs. The water bill alone ran into thousands…

The castle had always been a wealthy man's plaything. There had been hunting and fishing, some grazing land for the small herd of cows that had once supported the dairy, but there were no farms, no rents, no crops to support the estate.

There was no income other than what she could make with the B & B, craft workshops and the gardens. And the castle was on the far side of the creek, a ferry ride from the town. Fine for a visit, but it had to offer something special to tempt guests to stay.

Without the visitors to the gardens she would not survive. She had to make the most of them and Kam's idea of a wildflower walk with a picnic tea would be an excellent addition.

Maybe she could arrange some gardening talks? Lessons? Plant sales? Back in the days when there were gardeners, they'd boosted their meagre wages by selling plants they grew from cuttings, by division or from seed to visitors. She'd resisted opening a gift shop, but her roses were now with a grower who was producing them in quantity and a garden shop would be a good fit.

She jotted down ideas as they came to her, trying not to think about Kam and how he'd taken her into his arms to comfort her, the way he'd looked at her, kissed her.

She touched her lips, reliving the moment, then shook her head. Once before she'd been weak, stupid, thinking only of herself. This time she had to be strong for everyone at the castle. Kam's anger might have turned in a different direction, but he couldn't help her and his heart-melting kiss was a distraction she couldn't afford.

Easy to think, but it was hard to let go of a dream and she took Elizabeth Prideaux's cracked and fragile journal from the hidden drawer in her desk. Before she could open it the phone rang.

It was Joanne at the tourist office, calling to ask when they could put up the bluebell poster. She mentioned the idea of the wildflower walk and picnic and received an enthusiastic send-me-a-photograph-and-a-date response, which was cheering.

'Sorry, Kam,' she murmured as she ended the call. He'd made a fortune selling textiles; he could probably come up with dozens of ideas to help her sell the castle as a destination.

She wrote a note in her diary, checked the bookings for the following week, but his success story was nagging at her. How had he done that?

She'd glanced at a headline about two market traders creating an empire but couldn't understand why the story hadn't been picked up by the local paper and, unable to concentrate on anything else, she surrendered to curiosity and typed his name into the search engine.

There was no Kamal. There were, however, links to a KD Faulkner.

Was that him? Did Kam have a middle name? There had always been a tradition of Prideaux children having French names, but she had also been named for Elizabeth, who had lived in the castle before Henri ever set eyes on it. Who had held onto it after his death.

She placed her hand on her namesake's diary for a moment, then clicked on the first link. It was from one of the financial papers about the launch of an online company that had become a household name. She'd used it herself. She'd read a snippet in a homes and gardens magazine featuring a new bedding design at a special price. It had been exactly what she'd been looking for, for one of the B & B rooms in the castle.

She'd ordered a set, thinking that if it wasn't up to snuff she could send it back. What she'd actually done was buy more.

That was Kam's company?

How?

The article didn't say. It had been written in that typical low-key style favoured by the financial pages. It wasn't about the personalities, it was about the money. A lot of money. Everyone who worked for the company had been given shares as part of their salary and become wealthy overnight when it had gone public.

The two partners who'd founded it, former market traders, Raj Chowdry and KD Faulkner, had made a nine-figure fortune in the scramble for shares and still held more than fifty per cent of the stock.

She went back to the search engine, but it was just more of the same. There were no flashy photographs of nightclub celebrations in any of the lifestyle magazines. No brooding portraits of the new millionaires on the block in the Sunday supplements.

KD Faulkner and his partner had, it seemed, both chosen to keep a low profile, which was rare when everyone was on social media and being famous was the career choice of anyone over the age of five.

She checked social media. The company had a page, but not Kam. On the point of trying to dig deeper, she stopped and, feeling a little grubby, left the Internet and got on with some proper work.

'What about cats, Kam?' Barb asked. 'Sight hounds are hard-wired to go after cats.'

'There are no cats at the castle. Agnès is allergic to them.' She'd once been given a kitten and started wheezing within minutes of her first cuddle. She'd had no pets after that. The only animal had been Lady Jane's dachshund.

'So, you're not just down for a break to catch up with old friends, then? Support your favourite animal sanctuary?'

He'd spoken without thinking, and Barb, who'd made him work off the fees for his first dog by cleaning out the kennels—and who he'd gone back to help when he didn't have to—had been quick to pick up the slip.

'Where else would I go when I was looking for a dog?'

'I'm flattered, but shouldn't you check with Agnès first? I'm pretty sure they don't take pets at the castle and lurchers can be a handful.'

'I'm camping out,' he said. 'And I can handle Henry.' He'd got down on the floor so that he was on the dog's eye level. They shared a conspiratorial look and Henry leaned against him so that they were shoulder to shoulder, as if confirming that it was the two of them against the world. And cats.

'Henry?' She laughed. 'He had you from the moment you walked in, didn't he?'

'You had me. You lured me here with a photograph of a fit young Labrador and then put Henry in my path.'

She didn't deny it. 'He's very like the dog you had as a boy.'

'He has longer legs than Tramp.' His shaggy coat was a lighter mix of grey and white and there was a dark patch over his right eye that gave him a piratical look. It had been love at first sight. 'What's his background, Barb?' he asked, rubbing the dog's ear.

'We don't know. He was found wandering, all skin, bones and fleas. He's been cleaned up, had a full health check and all his shots. We've had him for a few months, so he's regained his weight. Normally I'd run a check on a new owner before I let a dog out of my charge, but I know you. He's good to go.'

'In other words, there was no rush to take him.'

'Not true. Quite a few people have fallen for him. He's got bags of character, a lovely nature, but there was the cat problem, and I cannot deny that he needs an experienced owner. I wouldn't let him go to just anyone.'

'You were waiting for me.'

'Maybe,' she said, laughing. 'It's good to see you back, Kam. Is your mother with you?'

'She prefers the sun. She runs cooking holidays from her home in Spain these days.'

'That sounds like a good life. Maybe she'll visit when you're settled?' He ignored the question. Thanks to his slip there was going to be enough speculation about his return to the castle, without him fuelling the gossip. ‘It was shocking what Sir Hugo did to you both,’ Barb continued, taking the hint. ‘And as for poor Agnès being left orphaned to be brought up by that dreadful man… I know I shouldn’t speak ill of the dead, but he led Lady Jane a shocking life with his affairs. The rumours about what went on on the island…’ She shook her head. ‘She hasn’t been well for years, poor lady, and now I hear that she’s in the early stages of Alzheimer’s.’

For the first time that day he was at a loss for words. Alzheimer’s? Why hadn’t Agnès said anything?

Stupid question. Why would she?

He’d come roaring in, treating her like the enemy, and she’d had her defences up.

Maybe they both had.

He gave Henry a last rub behind the ears and stood up.

Ten minutes later, all the paperwork completed, and everything a dog would need in a backpack with the rescue centre’s logo, he said, 'I'll remember you to my mother when I call her.'

'You do that. And thank you again for the donation. It will be put to good use.'

He nodded, looked down and said, 'Ready, Henry?'

He got an enthusiastic bark in response. The phone buzzed in Kam's jacket as they reached the door, but he ignored it. For the moment his total concentration had to be on the dog.

Henry trotted at his side, walking to heel, constantly looking up, constantly receiving reassurance. 'Good boy. Good boy, Henry.'

And Henry remained a good boy, walking tidily down the steps and along the quay until confronted with the dinghy. At which point he backed off and sat down.

'What? You're kidding me.' Henry gave a little whine in protest. Clearly he wasn't kidding. 'You're a lurcher, Henry. A poacher's dog. Intelligent, fearless, as happy in water as on dry land…'

Henry lay down, head flat on the ground between his paws, making himself as low as possible.

This wasn't the moment to push it. They were building a relationship, building trust, and the last thing he needed was to be in a small boat with a frantic dog. It was the last thing Henry needed.

'Okay, boy, let's try it another way.' He walked back up the steps and along to the ferry. Henry went rigid.

It wasn't, apparently, just small boats.

He could get a taxi but it was ten miles up the river to the nearest road bridge and a long way round to reach the castle from the other side. It was possible that Henry had never been in a car and there was no way of knowing how he'd react.

He'd sort this, but not today.

There was a narrow bridge a couple of miles up the creek that had been closed to traffic for years. Today it was going to be a long walk home.

He stopped to buy a couple of large bottles of water and snacks for them both and then called Agnès.

'Do you want lunch service, too?' she asked. 'Aren't the fish biting today?'

'What's today's special in the Orangery?'

'Fish pie.'

'I'll pass.'

'If that's all—'

'No. Wait!' She waited in silence. 'Is Tim about?'

'Tim?'

'I rowed over the creek this morning and, for reasons I won't go into now, I can't bring the dinghy back.'

'Are you hurt?' she asked, her voice softer, anxious. Was that concern?

'No, I'm fine. I just don't want to risk leaving the dinghy on the quay in case some idiot decides to take it for a joy ride.'

'As opposed to the idiot who took it for a joy ride this morning.' Forget the concern. 'Okay, leave it with me, I'll see to it.' And with that she ended the call.

'I think I'm in trouble, Henry.'

No doubt she thought he'd run into an old school friend and decided to go on a pub crawl. Or maybe she thought he'd run into a girl he'd known and they'd decided to catch up somewhere a little quieter.

Not his style, but she wasn't to know that.

His world had been the estate back then. The freedom of the woods, his dog, his guitar and Agnès.

It was late afternoon by the time he arrived back at the castle. He and Henry had taken it easy, enjoying the walk, taking water stops, taking detours through the woods to revisit old haunts, so that Henry could investigate interesting smells.

'What is that?'

He had just put one of the stainless-steel bowls he'd bought at the rescue centre on the steps of the castle and filled it with the last of the water from one of the bottles he'd bought, when Agnès appeared.

Henry was drinking noisily. Kam was drinking, rather less noisily, from his own bottle.

'It's not a what, it's a dog,' he said.

'Barely.' Agnès was glaring at him. 'If it isn't enough that you abandon a boat that you took without permission, you return with this…'

'Henry,' he said, since she was clearly lost for words.

'Henry?' And in that moment he realised

what he'd done. He'd taken one look at the dog and the name had seemed perfect. But Agnès had something against Henri Prideaux…

He didn't say the word that slipped into his brain, but he didn't need her chilly voice to know that he had done something really stupid and it was too late to do anything about it. The name was beyond recall.

It took her a moment, but she recovered sufficiently to say, 'It states clearly on our website that we don't accept dogs in the B & B. You are going to have to find other accommodation.'

She was *really* mad. Oddly that cheered him because that kind of reaction meant that what he did mattered to her.

And he was discovering that what she did mattered to him. A lot.

'You're missing a trick,' he said. 'Dog-friendly hotels are big business.'

'Are they? How interesting,' she said. 'In that case I'm sure you'll find somewhere suitable if you enter "dog hotel" in the search engine.'

'We'll camp out,' he said.

She hesitated then shrugged. 'I suppose he can't do much harm on the island. You know where to find the dinghy. You will be billed for my ferry fare and time.'

She'd gone herself?

'Doesn't Tim row?'

'It's Sunday. Tim is having roast beef and Yorkshire pudding at home with his mum.'

'Of course. I'm sorry to have inconvenienced you. I'll be happy with whatever charge you feel appropriate, however—' she narrowed her eyes at him '—I'm afraid the island won't be suitable.'

'Why?'

He had been afraid she would ask that. He just had to hope that he could make her laugh…

'You can't just take my word for it?' She crossed her arm and tapped a foot. Apparently not. 'Henry is afraid of boats.'

'That's ridiculous. Dogs love boats.'

'And so will Henry once I've discovered why he's scared.'

She frowned. 'How did you get back?'

'We walked.'

And there it was. She fought it, fought really hard, but the smile began in the depths of her eyes, little creases formed at their corners.

'That's got to be six miles,' she said.

'Nearer seven.'

Her mouth curved into a wide grin and then she was laughing, at first just a chuckle and then helplessly. Maybe there was a touch of hysteria. She finally pulled herself together, wiped her eyes and said, 'Thank you. I needed that. I imagine you could do with a cup of tea?'

'I thought you'd never ask.'

'You should get one at The Ferryside Inn. Fortunately they allow dogs in the bar.'

'Agnès!'

The smile was history. 'You called him Henry!' she declared, furiously. 'How could you?'

'Because I'm an idiot?' he suggested and got no argument. 'I'm sorry but he looked like a Henry. Maybe it was subconscious because he looks a bit like a pirate.'

'Henri Prideaux was a smuggler, not a pirate, but there's the irony. Your dog is frightened of boats.'

'You're right. It's hilarious. Now if someone could fetch my stuff from the island?'

'Fetch it yourself. You know where the dinghy is kept.'

'I begin to see why this B & B is not featured on the list of the hundred best places to stay in Devon.'

'You are not staying here, Kam. You are camping without permission on an island that is closed to the public on safety grounds. And now you have brought an unauthorised dog onto the estate.'

'You allow visitors to the garden to bring in dogs on leads,' he pointed out. 'What's the difference?'

'They walk round the woods and then go home!' She raised her hands in despair. 'Go away!'

'Okay,' he said. 'Henry, stay.'

Henry promptly sat, and it would have been an excellent demonstration of his obedience if Dora hadn't chosen that moment to skitter across the polished hall.

Henry shot after her like a rocket.

Agnès tried to grab him but he slipped through her hands and cornered Dora in the office where, from the safety of her retreat beneath the desk, she bared her teeth and gave a low, rolling growl.

Henry, confused, dropped to the floor, nose twitching in Dora's direction and, once again, Agnès laughed as Kam folded himself up beside Henry and held onto his collar.

There was definitely a touch of hysteria, he thought. This wasn't just about him and the dog. Something had happened. Not something good.

'Barb saw you coming, Kam.'

'Yes, she did,' he said. 'She remembered Tramp.'

'Tramp was shorter. And darker.' And the softness was back in her voice. 'He was a lovely old thing. I missed him.'

'So did I. We couldn't have dogs in the flat we were living in and, anyway, he would have hated the city. I took him to Battersea and they found him a home in the country with a great couple.'

All the anger seemed to leave her. 'How many times can I say I'm sorry, Kam?'

'I should have left him with you…' There were tears in her eyes and, unable to watch, he turned to Henry. 'Okay, you daft mutt, this is Dora. She's a dog, too. A very small, rather silly dog, but that's not her fault.'

'Not so silly.' Agnès sniffed, grabbed a tissue from her desk, blew her nose. 'She showed your useless mutt her teeth.'

'He just saw something small and furry and thought it was a cat.'

'Is that supposed to make me feel better?'

'No, I think that's going to take a while. But give these two a minute and they'll sort it out. Stay down, Henry. This is Dora's house.'

Henry put his head down, looking away from Dora, and gave a little whimper. She pushed her nose forward and gave a hesitant sniff.

It took a few minutes but Henry, with Kam's hand on his back, remained submissive and Dora finally had the confidence to trot out and give him a good sniff. By the time she'd finished, Henry, tired from his long walk, was asleep. Dora, satisfied that she had forced the newcomer to back down and submit, sat down and then curled up and followed suit.

'They'll be fine now,' he said, standing up.

'Will they?' She watched them for a moment and with her face in repose he could see the strain. Finally she looked up and said, 'Is it too early for gin?'

'I'll put the kettle on.'

'It doesn't have the same hit as a large gin.'

'No, but you won't feel so bad in the morning.'

'You think?' she muttered but followed him to the kitchen and slumped in a chair, making no move to help, or show him where things were.

He filled the kettle, found mugs, teabags, took the milk from the fridge. 'When did you last have something to eat?' he asked.

'I'm not hungry.'

'You look terrible.'

'So my grandmother keeps telling me.'

She'd put her hair up but there were strands escaping as if she'd been pushing her hands through it. She made an attempt to shove one back into place but it immediately fell back down. Giving up, she let her arms drop to the table and then laid her head on them.

She was at the end of her tether, he realised. Had probably been running on empty, not eating properly, for weeks.

'Is the boiler playing up again?' he asked. 'I could take a look—'

'No.' She struggled to sit upright. 'It's had its wobbly for the week.'

He found eggs and cheese in the fridge, washed his hands and then, as he cracked eggs into a basin, 'So I imagine this is about selling your mother's parure.'

'This?'

He gently whisked the eggs with a fork.

'How do you know about the parure?' The words were right but there was no punch to them. It was as if that scene on the steps had been a last gasp and the fight had gone right out of her. 'Have you been spying on me?'

He and Henry had taken a couple of water stops on the way home and, on one, he'd remembered the missed call.

He had no idea what a parure was and neither did his assistant, but it had been valued at a little under half a million pounds back in the nineteen-twenties. A valuation that had been conservatively increased by twenty-five per cent on her parents' death. An estimate. There had been no up-to-date valuation.

'So it's true? You are selling it?'

'Yes and no.'

'Which?' he asked, opening cupboards.

'What are you looking for?'

'The cheese grater.'

'Next one along. On your right.'

He found it, made tea in two mugs and put plenty of sugar in hers.

'So? Is it yes or no?' he said, as he set it in front of her and then set to work grating the cheese.

'I took it to an auction house in London yesterday. The jewellery man was out of the office so they said he would call me with a likely sale estimate when he'd seen it. He went in specially today.'

'I may be wrong but I'm getting the feeling that it wasn't good news.'

'There's good news and bad news. The good news is that I get to keep it. The bad news is that some time, in the last hundred years, someone replaced the diamonds with paste copies. Some Prideaux hard up for cash. Or maybe a crooked jeweller when it was sent for cleaning.

Or maybe not.' She propped her head on her hands as if it was too heavy to hold up by itself. 'Maybe they never were diamonds. Maybe it was all a con. The love story, the fabulous morning gift. The original bill of sale from the jewellers.'

'Unlikely,' he pointed out. 'There was a valuation in the nineteen-twenties.'

'You *have* been spying on me.'

'Wills are in the public record. You can download documents for a fee. Drink your tea.'

'You put sugar in it. I've never had sugar in my tea. Not even when I was a child.'

Of course not. This was cold comfort castle. Something he was determined to change.

'It will make you feel better.'

'It's going to take more than a spoonful of sugar in my tea,' she said, but she a took a sip. Then another one. 'And I had a call from the estate lawyer this afternoon. He's been very kind and he wanted to warn me that they expect the tax demand this week.'

'How long have you got?'

'They are going to negotiate staged payments.

A few months before the first one if I'm lucky but it's all academic.' She looked up. 'I spied on you, too. Well, I ran an Internet search. I wanted to know how you made all that money.'

'You couldn't wait for the book?'

'There isn't going to be a book. You are publicity shy.'

'I don't think my face on social media is going to sell one more bedding set.'

'You underestimate yourself.' Her blush brought some colour to her cheeks. What it did to him… 'I tried to find you on social media, too,' she said, 'but it made me feel grubby. Do you feel grubby, Kam?'

'Because I wanted to know what you had to sell? It's going to take a lot of money to put things right here,' he said. 'I was concerned you were throwing good money after bad.'

'I remember. You said. Well, no worries. There is no money, good or bad, to throw anywhere so I refer you to the question I asked earlier. Is it too early for gin?'

'Stick to the tea. As soon as I've finished this, I'll tell you my plan.'

'What does the D stand for?'

'D?'

'KD Faulkner.'

'Oh, that. It's David. My maternal grandfather's name.'

'I never heard you mention a grandfather. Is that where you went? When you left here?'

'I never met him or my grandmother. They disowned my mother when she became pregnant with an Arab immigrant.'

'I'm sorry,' she said, resting her chin on her hands. 'We haven't been lucky on the grandparent front, have we?'

'What about your mother's parents?'

'They were quite old when she was born. I don't think they got over losing her. I put having a baby in my five-year plan. I don't want to leave it too late.'

His hand slipped and he took a piece of skin off his knuckle with the cheese grater.

'A baby? Another generation to keep the Prideaux clan at bay?'

'No. A child who will grow up to be her own person. No strings, no ties, no expectations, just loved.'

'Her?' He had a sudden image of a small girl,

the image of Agnès, running wild and free on the estate, but loved, cherished. Teaching her to swim, as he'd taught her mother…

'Or him. You're bleeding into the cheese.'

He swore under his breath, crossed to the sink, ran cold water over his hand then grabbed a piece of kitchen paper to wrap around it before opening the first-aid box.

'You could bleed to death while you're trying to open these things,' he said, trying to rip open a dressing with his teeth.

Agnès stood up, took it from him, opened it and, having removed the paper towel, bent over to examine the wound. Then she placed the dressing carefully over the cut and smoothed it into place with her fingers, holding his hand for a moment, checking her handiwork.

'Will I live?' he asked and when she looked up to answer him, her mouth was just inches from his. Soft, pink, slightly open so that there was a glimpse of white teeth.

If he leaned forward a few inches he could kiss her again and, this time, if she kissed him back, they could take their time about it and discover if the attraction he felt for this new, grown-up version of the Agnès he'd fallen in love with would find an answering echo.

CHAPTER SEVEN

The parure is a bust. I am bust. Where are the matches?
Agnès Prideaux's Journal

'IT'S JUST A SCRATCH.'

Agnès, head spinning, took a step back.

Kam had been going to kiss her again and every cell in her body had been screaming for her to lean in to him and take the initiative. Show him how much she wanted that.

Like that had worked so well before.

There had been half a dozen times since he'd been back when they had seemed to be hovering on the threshold of a kiss but one or other of them had taken a step back.

The kiss on the island hadn't been like that. It had been no more than a reaction to her outburst. For a moment she had allowed herself to respond but had torn herself away before she had betrayed herself utterly.

Kam hadn't come back for her.

He'd made no secret of the fact that he blamed her for what had happened to him and his mother, that it was his avowed intention that she should lose her home at his hand, as he had done at hers.

The realisation that he couldn't buy it had forced him to reconsider. He'd softened towards her, apparently sharing her concerns, but there was nothing here for him except the chance to achieve some kind of closure by finishing what she had started.

She couldn't afford that kind of self-indulgence.

'You left your bag on the step,' she said, needing to escape before she flung herself at him like the desperate teenager she had once been. 'I'll bring it in. Check on the dogs.'

'Leave it. No one is going to run off with a bag of dog food. I'll pick it up later and if you've never heard the phrase let sleeping dogs lie…'

Kam cleared away the tainted cheese, lifted

down an omelette pan that was hanging from the overhead rack, turned on a burner.

'Bread?'

'In the larder.' He raised an eyebrow. 'You want me to get it?'

'I've got my hands full. Don't forget the butter.'

'Eggs, cheese, butter… Can your heart take it?'

'I rowed across the creek and I've walked seven miles today. I think my heart could do with a break, don't you?'

There it was again, that look, that connection. It grew with each exchange, with each smile, each touch.

It would be so easy and maybe, if the stars lined up, the baby would be a small version of him, grow into a boy to run wild in the woods like his father. Who she could teach to fish and swim, the way he'd taught her.

No. Just no.

This wasn't about the past. Every moment of discord, every half-smile, teasing moment, touch laid down a new memory, some bitter, some sweet, but all risking a deeper hurt.

She fetched the bread, took butter from the fridge, filled a jug with water, laid out a knife and fork for him while Kam, very efficiently, created a fluffy cheese omelette that he broke in half and divided between two plates he'd taken from the warming rack.

He placed one in front of her, the melted cheese oozing out.

'Oh, I didn't realise…' He'd cooked for her? 'Who taught you to cook?'

'My mother.' He cut two thick slices of bread from the loaf, buttered them generously and handed a slice to her. 'She considers it an essential life skill.'

'How is she, Kam?'

'She's well. She has a *finca* in Spain where she runs cooking classes.'

It was the first information he'd volunteered, she realised.

'How often do you see her?'

'Every month or so. She has a great many friends and has a good life. One would like to be more, but she values her independence. She won't allow him to move in.'

'I'm glad she's happy. My grandmother said something today…'

Realising that she wasn't eating, he handed her his fork. 'Eat,' he said, leaning back to take another one from the cutlery tray.'

'Yes. Thank you.'

Kam watched to make sure she was obeying him, then said, 'What did your grandmother say?'

'Her memory isn't that great these days, she rambles, but I told her that you were here. In case she saw you,' she added, quickly. 'She remembers your mother. That she liked her…' She hesitated, remembering his sarcasm about the word 'treasure'.

Kam looked at her. 'And?'

'She said that my grandfather liked her, too, but that she wouldn't…'

He frowned. 'Wouldn't what?'

'Wouldn't be nice to him.'

'Nice?' He stilled, fork halfway to his mouth, then lowered it. 'Are you suggesting that he expected *droit de seigneur*?'

'I don't know.'

'Yes, you do.' He swore, put the fork down.

'It was never about us, was it? He didn't give a fig about you.'

'It's still my fault, Kam. If I hadn't…' She let the sentence trail off, unwilling to say the words out loud. To bring that moment into the daylight.

Kam had no such compunction. 'If you hadn't swum naked over to the island with the sole purpose of seducing me, he wouldn't have had an excuse to get rid of her?'

She had shrunk from saying the words, from even thinking them but, despite all the vile things her grandparents had said, she had nothing to be ashamed of. She had loved him. She had wanted to give him, not just her heart, but her body so that he would know how much she loved him.

'He would have found one sooner or later,' she said, 'but I handed it to him on a plate.'

'*We*, Agnès. You weren't alone out there. I had my hand on you but he didn't care about that. Any other man would have turned on me, lashed out, and we both know that he had a violent temper. He was carrying a stick and I expected a beating but he just told you to go home and waited to make sure you obeyed him. He didn't even look at me. He just turned and walked back to the summer house. That kind of control is a lot more terrifying than violence. I didn't know what to do. I wanted to follow you to make sure you were all right but thought that would only make things worse. In the end I went home and told my mother what had happened. She was already packing when he turned up at the door next morning.'

'I don't know what to say.'

'Nothing. You don't have to say anything. He didn't get angry because we had given him exactly what he wanted.'

We, she thought, was the most beautiful word in the English language. In any language, and she sat watching him, as he sliced into the egg with his fork as if nothing had happened, trying, without success, to control a grin that was doing its best to break out.

He glanced up and smiled back. 'Don't let it get cold.'

'No,' she said, and ate every scrap.

When they had finished he cleared the plates, stacked them in the dishwasher, wiped the omelette pan with kitchen paper and then sat back down beside her.

'Are you feeling better?'

'Yes. Thank you. I'm sorry I was such a cow about Henry. He can sleep wherever he likes.'

She was half on her feet, when he caught her hand. 'Don't run away.'

'I wasn't. Running. I have to sort out the rooms for the weekend guests. Make a laundry list. Pay some bills—'

'The laundry will wait, and, as for the bills, I have a proposition for you.'

'We've been through all this.'

'Just listen to me. You owe me that.'

'I thought we were past owing each other anything,' she said. She would always hold herself responsible, but with that 'we' he'd forgiven her.

'Let's say we owe each other.'

She sank back down onto the chair.

'First let me tell you what I want to do here.' She opened her mouth to tell him that it was pointless. 'You can have your say when I'm done.'

She raised a hand a few inches, as if to say it was a waste of time, but she would hear him out.

'I lived in some pretty appalling areas after we left here.' His turn to hold up a hand when she would have interrupted. 'This is not about blame. No more apologies. The past is the past.

'I don't need to spell out the dangers that inner city kids run every day of their lives. You see the worst of it every night on the news.'

'You?' she asked.

'If I'd been a different boy maybe, but I knew something different. I knew that there was another life. And I knew how to be quiet, how to be invisible and I mostly stayed out of trouble.'

'You did a lot more than that.'

'Because of what I'd learned. I want to give that chance to some kids. Bring them here and show them more than concrete and graffiti.'

'How did you survive?' she asked.

'I couldn't fish to make money so I made myself useful at the market, working before college, at the weekends, helping with the set-up. At first I just worked for tips but then Raj gave me a job.'

She hadn't meant that. She meant how had

he survived in such an alien environment, but she supposed it was the same thing.

'On the clothing stall?' she prompted. 'I saw a photograph. When I looked online. It was in one of the financial papers.'

He nodded. 'Raj had a decent business. He was bringing in good quality stuff from his cousin's factory in India that attracted, not just the locals, but people with the money to shop in Knightsbridge. How they found out about us, goodness only knows.'

'The market is famous. Big companies, banks, have offices in the area. It only takes one woman at a loose end, while she's waiting for a husband or lover who works in one of those city offices, a woman who works in one herself maybe, to spend her lunch hour browsing the stalls. She tells a friend about an amazing little stall where she found a bargain, who tells someone else… There's nothing like word of mouth. You're the man with the millions, you should know this.'

'I understand about word of mouth, but it's that first one… I hope whoever she met makes her happy.'

'I hope she's CEO of a bank.'

He laughed. 'Yes.'

'You sold shares in more than a market stall. How did you go from that to an Internet phenomenon?'

'A woman—not in designer clothes, but smart—started coming early several times a week, choosing one or two items of baby and young kids clothing and buying them in every size. It was obvious what she was doing and, London traffic being what it is, I had no trouble following her on my bike. She had a smart little children's boutique where she was relabelling and selling our stuff on for five times the price.'

'What? That's outrageous.'

'My thoughts precisely. I asked my mother to go in and buy something, so I had the label and the price tag to show Raj. He'd made his profit and shrugged it off, but I could see that he could be making a lot more money.'

'Clearly he could put up the prices,' she said.

'No.' He shook his head, then realised she was kidding and grinned. 'No, but I put together a plan, made a spreadsheet to show him how much he could be making if he went online.'

'Not a hard sell.'

'You'd think not, but he was making a good living and he didn't want the bother, or the risk. People will always cling to their comfort zone unless you give them a very good reason to move. In the end I told him he could carry on doing exactly what he was doing. That I'd set up the online business, but I wanted sixty per cent of it.'

'Sixty?'

'The risk was all mine and I could have gone direct to his cousin and cut a deal with him.'

'And now you're going to sell your plan to me.'

'I get the feeling that it will take more than a spreadsheet.'

'It will take a miracle, but I interrupted you telling me how smart you are.' His look suggested he was not taken in by her change of subject. 'No, seriously. I'm interested.'

He shrugged. 'I found a smart IT student who built a website for peanuts and shares in the company, then I set up media pages, started posting pictures of what we were selling alongside pictures of the same stuff in the boutique.'

'How did the boutique owner take that?'

'She was furious but she went on buying from Raj until he closed the stall so presumably she was still selling to her niche market.' Agnès shook her head. 'I contacted mummy bloggers, sent them free stuff to review with the message, why pay West End prices when you could buy exactly the same thing direct at a fraction of the price?'

'Clearly it worked.'

'It was slow at first but we gradually gathered momentum and then one of the mother and baby magazines I'd targeted ran a paragraph with a picture of a very sweet dress and before we knew it we were renting a warehouse instead of a lock-up. Now we have three factories, and total control means that we can offer decent wages, safe working conditions and health benefits for the men and women who work for us.'

'Doesn't that push up the price of production?'

'It's all a matter of scale. We're about to expand into—'

'No. Stop.' She shook her head. 'Please, stop.' She'd heard enough.

'You have a question?'

'No.' She didn't know what she had except that she'd had a really bad day and he was sitting there telling her how clever he'd been, how well he'd done. 'You've said enough.'

'You did ask.'

'I know, but here's a thing, Kam. You were angry with me when you left,' she said. 'Really angry. It's okay, I get it. You'd just been turfed out of your home. But you were still angry with me when you came back a few days ago. You were rude, you wanted to humiliate me, wanted to evict me from my home the way my grandfather evicted you from yours. All that "revenge is a dish best served cold" stuff.'

'I was—'

'Normally, I'd say that when you carry anger that long,' she continued, as if he hadn't spoken, 'you are the only one it hurts.'

'What I'm trying to say—'

'I'm not finished, Kam.' She waited and after

a moment he gestured for her to continue. 'You talked about having to force Raj Chowdry out of his comfort zone but how comfortable were you?'

He frowned. 'I don't—'

'That was a rhetorical question.'

This time he held up his hands in a gesture of surrender.

'You had the entire estate to run wild in, as much cash as you needed from the fish you poached, everything you ever wanted without a whit of responsibility. You said it yourself. Everything you've done was to bring you a step closer back to Castle Creek.'

His face was stony now, but she'd lived with the guilt for years and at that moment all she was feeling was fury.

'The truth is, Kam, that I did you the world's biggest favour. If you had stayed here you wouldn't be a multimillionaire and heading for billionaire. You would still be cutting the grass.'

'Like hell I would.'

Her turn to raise her eyebrows and he had the grace to return a slightly rueful smile. 'Okay, but I'd be getting paid for it. And running private side excursions for visitors who wanted to visit the smugglers' cave.'

'You think it would sell?'

'You'd need someone who could tell a good story.'

She shook her head. 'I've heard enough. Since you can't return to the island, I will concede the point and allow Henry to stay in your room tonight, but you need to find alternative accommodation tomorrow.'

'Don't you want to hear my offer, Agnès? Or are you going to keep running away?'

'I'm not running. I'm walking.'

'It's not the speed, it's the intention. What are you afraid of?'

'I'm not afraid, I'm being realistic. This isn't a market stall and I'm not a trader who's happy just getting by. There is nothing you can do here.'

'I can pay your tax bill, your debts. I can have the castle roof, and anything else, repaired and have a new boiler installed. I can save your home for you, Agnès. All I want in return is to live in my old home, which I will renovate and extend, and the chance to help some kids turn their life around.'

'I thought you wanted to own the land you walk on. The roof over your head.'

'Maybe that isn't as important as I thought.'

'And the castle? I thought you wanted that.'

'I want to be able to use the land, the woods, the creek. You are welcome to the castle.'

She wanted to hear more, to listen to his plans, say yes, please to his offer and tell him he could do anything. But it wouldn't do.

'It's a noble project and I wish you well with it. Unfortunately, it won't be here. I can't accept your offer.'

He looked stunned, as well he might be. She'd just turned down a seven-figure gift.

'You're turning me down flat?'

'One of us has to be sensible and I've clearly had more experience. While you've been building an empire, I've been dealing with drains, dodgy boilers, putting buckets under leaky roofs, taking care of my grandmother.'

'I'm offering to make all that go away.'

'I know, but you're allowing emotion, sentiment, to get in the way of common sense. You could sink a fortune into the castle, the estate, but if a drunk driver sent my car flying off the road and into the creek, if I fell under a bus in Market Street, if the branch of a tree fell on my head as I was walking through the wood, you would have nothing. The money would be spent and Pierre Prideaux wouldn't be taking on a castle in dire straits, he would be the beneficiary of your generosity. You'd have no claim, no rights and, for the second time in your life, you would be turfed out of Creek Cottage.'

'I realise that and I've got a solution.'

'Give it up, Kam—'

'Marriage,' he said, cutting her off. 'We can get married. Unless there's someone else in your life?'

It was her turn to freeze. Words, dozens of them, were tumbling from her brain—yes, no, please, crazy, yes—but thankfully her mouth was refusing to co-operate, her jaw locked tight.

The man would clearly do anything to get what he wanted, even marry her. It was extreme but he wasn't the first to come up with the idea. Unfortunately, he had the wrong name.

She took a long slow breath. She just had to keep calm and keep saying no.

'What was it about the entail that you didn't understand, Kam?'

'I understood it perfectly. The castle can only be inherited by someone who is born here at the castle, or it goes to Henri's Norhou family.'

'Ten out of ten for attention. I think that concludes our discussion.'

'Not quite. If we were married, Agnès, a child would be a logical conclusion. In the fullness of time, he or she would inherit.'

A child?

He could never own the castle, but his child, their child, could?

'You're thinking long term,' she managed through the lump that had materialised in her throat.

'Priddy Castle has been here a long time.'

Her mouth was dry; breathing was a physical effort. A baby, Kam's baby, was a combination of her wildest dream and worst nightmare and she didn't know how to react, what to say.

'Do you want time to think it over?' he asked.

How much time would make her answer any

easier? He was offering her everything she'd ever wanted, except the one thing she wanted above everything.

'A marriage of convenience,' she finally managed. 'Money and property. My grandfather would approve.'

'Is that a yes?'

'I never did anything he approved of yet,' she said.

'Then marry me and it's a win-win.'

'For me,' she said. 'It's still a gamble for you. You should have proof of fertility before putting your millions at risk.'

'We could give it a try, if it will make you feel better, but, even assuming we get as lucky as your parents, it's going to take nine months to produce the goods. I don't think you have that much time.'

There was a hollow feeling below her ribs. An emptiness. He was right, of course, but for a moment she had been overwhelmed with longing. If she couldn't have his heart, she would at least have the joy of his child quickening inside her.

'No, there's not much time,' she said, pushing the thought away. 'I have so many ideas. If I could just get my head above water…'

'I will keep you afloat, Agnès.'

His voice was gentle, reassuring. He reached out, inviting her to take his hand, accept what he was offering. Selling it to her with gentle words.

'I need some air.' She pushed her chair back and stumbled from the table. 'A lot of air,' she said, when he made a move to follow.

She bolted for the back door, grabbing her coat from the mud room, running across the courtyard, past the old dairy and buttery that were now the craft workshops, through the stable yard.

She veered away from the kitchen garden. If he came after her, the greenhouse was the first place he would look. He knew all the places she'd hidden when things became unbearable. He knew everything about her, except that she had once loved him. Could have loved him again…

She slowed. Who did she think she was kidding? She had never stopped loving him, never stopped hoping that one day he would come back. It was why she had flat out refused to go to London and 'do the season'. She wasn't looking for a new love; she'd been in love since she was three years old and had spotted the nearly five-year-old Kam trailing after his father as he'd cut the grass. She didn't want a new love because in her heart, in her head, she wasn't done with the old one.

His return had not been the required fairy-tale ending, but then she had always hated fairy tales. She lived in a castle and knew the cold reality.

She stopped. Her legs were shaking and she sank onto a bench and tried to control her ragged breathing, to slow down the rapid beating of her heart.

Her last-ditch attempt to save the day had failed, the tax man was at the door and Kam had offered her the bargain of a lifetime. Why had she even hesitated? There were too many lives at stake to get precious over the fact that this had nothing to do with how he felt about her, everything about his feelings for the place where he grew up.

Running away like this was ridiculous, embarrassing, but she needed time alone to rationalise her decision. At the moment Kam was setting out what he was prepared to pay to get what he wanted. No more than he'd pay if he'd been able to buy the estate and this way he'd have a partner he knew he could rely on to run the castle, the gardens… He wouldn't ever own it himself, but it would be like having a lifetime lease.

Her mobile pinged. It was a text from Suz.

Mr Faulkner asked me to tell you that he's taken both the dogs for a walk. Do you want to tell me what's going on?

She groaned. He'd seen her run and was letting her know that it was safe to come back. Could it be any more embarrassing? Could her day get any worse?

Without a doubt. He had given her a couple of hours' thinking time, which, considering his generosity, should be plenty. Why was she even hesitating?

But somehow it felt like a game of hide and

seek and sooner, rather than later, he was going to be coming for his answer, ready or not.

She had to go to the one place he couldn't follow her.

Having promised Suz that there was nothing to worry about, assured her that she'd explain everything later, Agnès left her in charge for the night and half an hour later she was tying up at the dock on the island.

She'd brought food, warm clothes, kindling and quickly got a fire going in the stone circle that Kam had built. She pulled out the tarpaulin and found a quiet pleasure in making a camp, building a bivouac, doing things she used to do with Kam and had not done since he'd left.

She filled a kettle with the water she had brought with her and set it on the fire and then she opened her tablet and did what she always did when there was a decision to be made.

She made a list of the pros and cons.

There was a long list of pros.

He wanted access to the estate so that he could give inner city kids a glimpse of another life, maybe internships with his company, the chance of further education.

They were good things, things she could be proud to be a part of. With the extra money available when she wasn't spending every penny on keeping the castle watertight and barely ticking over, she would be able to help more youngsters like Suzanna. Offer them a place of safety with a chance to build a worthwhile and rewarding life.

The prospect excited her in a way nothing had done for a very long time. Until Kam had walked into her office and jump-started all kind of impossible thoughts, thoughts that had been as quickly stopped by his manner.

Her heart might have been pounding, but he had been all business. Now, faced with the reality of the entail, he'd decided that marriage was the only way to get what he wanted.

Marriage and a child to give him a personal stake in the castle. She had to give him credit, it was a good plan, although whoever had run the check at the probate office hadn't realised that the child did not have to be the result of a legal union.

She wasn't about to tell him that. Marriage would give her rights and a settlement should he become bored with his convenient marriage and decide to seek more interesting companionship. There would be plenty of women happy to amuse a multimillionaire.

She swallowed down a large lump in her throat.

She'd made a list of the pros. What were the cons?

He didn't love her.

She loved him.

Everything and nothing but then her mother was probably the first bride to come to the castle purely for love.

She would only be doing what Prideaux women, Prideaux men, had been doing for centuries and marrying for the benefit of the estate.

Kam cursed himself for a fool, but anger had blinded him. He'd arrived all fired up with self-righteous indignation, blaming Agnès for their banishment when the clock had already been counting down. If it hadn't been her, it would have been something else.

In all that time, seeing his mother working three jobs to keep body and soul together, missing out on his education, university, he hadn't given a thought to what Agnès might have suffered.

She'd had plans, had her heart set on studying horticulture like her mother. Instead she'd been stuck here with her bully of a grandfather, caring for a sick grandmother who had never given her the love she deserved.

She hadn't buckled.

Denied her choice of career, she had retaliated by defying the old man's plans to marry her off to money. How ironic that she must now see it as her only hope.

Kam hadn't thought of it that way. He hadn't thought about it at all or he wouldn't have tossed out his proposal so carelessly.

Marriage was a big deal and yet, at that moment, sitting together in the old kitchen, it hadn't seemed like a leap into the unknown, but the most natural thing in the world. They both loved the castle, the estate, wanted to keep it a special place. As partners they could have it all and when he'd countered her argument with a baby, a light had shone from her eyes. At that point he'd thought he was there.

But this was Agnès. Stubborn as a mule Agnès.

He smiled despite everything. He'd fallen in love with her that last disastrous summer, but that had just been the physical manifestation of a love that had happened long before that. When she'd threaded maggots on hooks for him day after day because until she'd done that a hundred times he wouldn't teach her to fish. When he'd hauled her out of the creek, floundering, blue with cold, but refusing to give up until she could swim to the island. When he'd stayed with her in the greenhouse to feed a baby hedgehog around the clock with an eye-dropper because she'd refused to let it die.

That was why, with just weeks to find money for the taxman or lose the castle, he knew his stubborn Agnès would accept his inept proposal. She'd rationalise it as her duty to keep the estate from developers, to take care of the people who relied on her for their home, for their livelihood and, in some cases, their safety. And maybe, when she'd forgiven him for how he'd acted when he'd arrived, just a little bit because she had once loved him enough to risk her grandfather's wrath.

And while she was getting to that he'd do everything in his power to show her that she wouldn't have to close her eyes and think of Priddy Castle but open them and see that marriage to him would be an adventure.

He'd taken the dogs along the beach, hoping that Dora would show Henry that boats were nothing to fear, but the dinghy was missing.

He sat for a while on a rock, looking across at the island, hating that she'd felt the need to distance herself from him, finally understanding what had driven Agnès to strip off and swim out to him.

The temptation to follow her lead was strong but he had to give her time. This wasn't the moment for dramatic gestures or declarations that she had no reason to believe. Telling someone you loved them was meaningless. You had to show them.

The first thing he could do was sort out the Orangery but before he could do that he needed to see the contract.

As soon as he got back to the castle and had settled the dogs, he went to Agnès's office. There was an old book lying on her desk and he was about to pick it up when Suzanna appeared in the doorway.

'Oh. I didn't realise there was anyone here. If you're looking for Agnès—'

'No.' She waited. 'I'm looking for the catering contract for the Orangery. From some of the things Agnès told me, I'm pretty sure that she has grounds to renegotiate it. Maybe even cancel it.'

'I'm sure she'll show it to you when she returns.' She had been polite but was clearly suspicious at finding him alone in the office.

'Without a doubt, but I'd rather not get her hopes up without good reason.'

Suzanna shook her head. 'It just about broke her heart when Agnès saw what they were doing. She thought they had listened to her ideas, but they were just humouring her and once she'd signed… That man at the bank wants locking up.'

'That's the first place to apply pressure,' he agreed, 'but I will need the contract.'

'I shouldn't…' He waited. 'Can you really do something?' He waited some more and then she crossed to a cabinet and removed a file, clutching it to her chest, as if still unsure.

'I'll take a copy,' he said. 'Agnès will never know I've seen it unless I can fix things.'

'She said your mother used to work here,' she said, still reluctant to hand over the file, 'but I've never heard her mention your name but it's obvious you have history.'

History. A good word. And a future, if he was lucky. 'We do. I've known her since she was three and spent my early life leading Agnès astray.'

'So you were friends.' Agnès had never talked about him—and why should she?—but that seemed to satisfy Suzanna and she handed over the file. 'I hope you can fix this.'

'I'll do my best.'

'Right,' she said.

She was backing out of the tiny office when he said, 'Agnès told me she's trying to get your sister here.'

'Yes. She's growing up…' And then she broke down in tears.

CHAPTER EIGHT

A marriage of convenience, for heaven's sake. It's the twenty-first century but nothing, it seems, has changed if you're a Prideaux woman. The fact that I love him should make it easier, but he doesn't love me so it's much, much worse.
Agnès Prideaux's Journal

AGNÈS TRIED TO IGNORE the ringing of her phone, but when she checked the caller ID she saw that it was Suzanna, and she wouldn't call without good reason.

'Suz? Is there a problem?'

'No problem. I just wanted to make sure you were okay.'

Kam!

'You borrowed Suz's phone! Is she okay?' she asked, quickly.

'She's fine. I told her I wanted a quick word

with you, but that my phone was out of charge and she was kind enough to let me use hers to call you. You wouldn't have answered if you'd thought it was me, would you?'

'Probably not,' she admitted. 'You are a distraction when I'm trying to focus on…on the future. I needed space to think.'

'You chose a good place to do that but focus on the good things we can do together. Who knows, I might find you another potential Tim. That boy would make a great mentor.'

She softened. 'I'm glad you see his great qualities. I thought that I might set up a proper internship programme. If any of your young people wanted to try the life here, in the garden, the woods or the hotel. Provide some basic training in job skills. Perhaps your company could offer bursaries for those wanting to go on to higher education?'

'We are going to make a great team, Agnès.'

A team? Not exactly what she'd hoped for, but if they could keep it impersonal, focus on the castle, the business, the young people they both cared about, have a shared purpose, then the missing element might not be such a yawning gap in their marriage. And that was the next item on her list.

'A wedding in the chapel, a reception in the dining room, would be great for business,' she added.

'A wedding? Are you going to break the habit of a lifetime and do something of which your grandfather would approve?'

'You think he'd approve?'

'You told me you were expected to marry for money.'

His words stung, as she was sure they were meant to, and she responded in kind.

'I was,' she replied, 'but if you imagine, Kam, that wealth would have made you acceptable to him in any way, think again.'

Agnès wanted to call the words back the moment they left her mouth, but Kam just laughed. 'I have no illusions. The bigoted old bastard will be turning in his grave at the thought of the two of us together.'

Despite everything, she found herself grinning at this glimpse of the old closeness. It had once been the two of them against the world. Invincible. For a moment it felt that way again.

'In this instance,' he said, 'we both win.'

Win?

Reality check.

Kam was driven by what had happened to him in the past. His plan to help disadvantaged inner city kids could have been accomplished anywhere but it had to be the castle. Since it couldn't happen without her, he'd incorporated her into the plan. She must never forget that.

'It's been a long time, Kam. Whatever was between us is way back in the mists of time.'

He didn't rush to deny it but said, 'Time is the one thing we don't have.'

'I'm not suggesting we delay the wedding. Just…' She swallowed. 'You've come back from a long way away, Kam. Not just distance, but from a different life. You are not the boy who left here. I'm not the girl you left behind.' How much more plainly could she put it? 'We need time to re-establish a relationship.'

'We're doing that with every word we speak, every plan we make for the future of the castle.'

'That's it,' she said, grabbing for something solid to hang onto. 'It's all about the castle. You want it. I need to save it. Where are *we* in all that?'

The words came out in a rush. Making it personal. Exactly what she'd been determined to avoid.

'Are you saying that you need time before you're prepared to have a baby with me?'

She was sitting in the darkness, with only the light from her phone and the campfire, and his voice was so soft, so intimate in her ear that if he were here, if he were with her, nothing would have stopped her from flinging herself at him, making the body and soul commitment she'd been on the threshold of all those years ago. From saying those three dangerous words…

When the silence had gone on for too long, he said, 'I understand, Agnès. There will be a lot of work to be done here and I think it would be sensible to close the castle for a while so that you can relaunch it with a new website later in the year. We should leave Suz in charge and go away for a while after the wedding.'

'Away? No. I can't leave—'

'I have to go to India in a few weeks,' he said,

ignoring her protest. 'Everyone would expect you to come with me on honeymoon.'

Agnès felt her heart go thump, the hot flush of desire that had been hovering on the brink since he'd walked into her office flood through her veins. How easy it would be to surrender, say to him, 'Come to me now.'

Easy for the girl she had once been. For the woman she'd become it was the hardest thing in the world because in the moment she succumbed to that hunger she would be his. There would be no going back.

She took a steadying breath. Her voice had to be strong. There could be no betraying wobble…

'I can't—'

'It's just a word. A show for the world at large,' he replied, equally calm, 'and, if I'm honest, a little for pride. How will it look if I go away straight after the wedding and you stay behind?'

What was that? A tiny chink in his confidence? She felt an unexpected rush of affection for this man who had everything, everything except the one thing that only she could give him.

It was something beyond physical desire. And far more dangerous.

'You will love India.'

'Will I?' It was true that the word held some magic enchantment.

'I know your world, Agnès. I'm suggesting I show you mine. Apart from anything else I think you could do with a break. You've had a rough year. Getting away for a while will give you a new perspective, maybe some inspiration. If nothing else, come for the colour, the gardens, to lie in the sun. We can get to the rest when you're ready.'

India… Exotic, colourful, warm nights and sea breezes. She could feel her limbs melting at the thought. Falling for the temptation.

And with the temptation came the doubt.

Kam had built an empire by selling his idea, selling himself, selling a lifestyle. He was selling himself to her right now. Using what he knew about her.

The gardens had been a clever touch. He knew that plants had been her passion, that she'd wanted to follow her mother into horticulture.

Was that how the women in her family had coped with marriage to men who had only married them so that they could give them a son, or, failing that, a daughter to inherit the castle?

Had they subsumed their deepest longings into passion for their gardens, the creation of exquisite needlework, collecting things with which to fill their empty lives while their children were taken care of by nursemaids and nannies?

Clearly there had been affection, even love, in some of those marriages, but there were some that had been beastly affairs, including that of her poor grandmother.

Kam was all sweetness and light now, but he'd been bitingly angry when he'd arrived. How would he be once she'd given him what he wanted? He had come back looking for revenge and what could be sweeter than to marry the last Prideaux of Priddy Castle in order to claim it for himself?

He was showing her his caring side now, going along with all her ideas, but once he had an heir and the estate was, effectively, his, she would have served her usefulness. He could divorce her in a year or two and still have everything he wanted.

He would undoubtedly want a prenup to protect his wealth. Well, she would have one, too. There was no money to protect, but there was her pride.

'I want you to have your heir, Kam. It's all I can give you in return for what you're doing for me, for the people I care about, but—'

'Agnès—'

'I can't—'

'Agnès,' he said, a little more sharply, demanding her attention and then, when he had it, 'I have a copy of the entail. I know we don't have to be married for our child to inherit but I want you to know that I am fully committed to a partnership with you.'

'Oh…' The words that had been bursting out of her mouth were suddenly stuck in her throat. He knew, and yet he was still proposing marriage. Tears were stinging the backs of her eyes and she had to blink hard to stop them from falling.

He was still selling himself as Mr Nice Guy.

She might have adored him as a girl, but he hadn't always been a nice boy.

He'd once left her stuck up a tree he'd dared her to climb, abandoning her to go off and do some boy thing that he hadn't wanted her to be part of. And while she'd been thrilled to be his accomplice when he'd had fish to sell, he'd been using her because he'd known that if the warden had stopped her, he might have confiscated the fish, but he wouldn't have risked a confrontation with her grandfather.

'Do you want my gratitude?' she asked, more sharply than she'd intended.

'No!' He sounded hurt.

'That was another rhetorical question, Kam. Anything but marriage would have been a deal breaker,' she said, even if she had her fingers mentally crossed as she said it. 'I was going to say that I am happy to have your heir as soon as possible, but that a honeymoon baby doesn't need an actual honeymoon. There are other ways.'

This time the silence was longer.

'You're planning on the turkey-baster option?' he asked, when she thought he would never speak again. 'Is that why you're hiding out on the island? Did you think I would try to force myself on you?' His voice was hard now.

'No!' He'd cared about her, cooked for her and she'd run because she'd wanted him to hold her, wanted him to make love to her. 'No, Kam. And I'm not hiding. I just needed somewhere peaceful to think.'

'And I have disturbed you.' Beyond imagining… 'What conclusion did you reach?'

She swallowed. 'That I'd be more comfortable with…with what you said.' If she hadn't loved him, it wouldn't matter. But to give herself to him so totally and discover that he was playing her would destroy her. 'You are so clear what you want,' she rushed on, a little desperately, before he could answer. 'I had to work out what I need.'

'And, apart from the turkey baster, what have you decided?' His voice was even, controlled.

He was getting everything he wanted, she reminded herself. She wasn't being unreasonable, not that he was suggesting that she was. However, a reserve had entered his voice.

She tried to speak, had to clear her throat before she could answer.

'I'm working on it.'

'Text me a list when you're done. It doesn't have to be exhaustive. I'm not going to say that if it's not on the list you can't have it. I want this to work for both of us.'

This was ghastly. Embarrassment off the scale. 'Kam…'

'The main reason I rang is to tell you that I have to go to London tomorrow.'

He was brisk now, matter-of-fact as he cut her off. Just as well— she had no idea what she could say.

I want you so much my bones ache?

He talked of pride. She was hanging onto hers by a thread.

'Since we have to give twenty-eight days' clear notice of marriage,' he continued, 'I suggest we go to the register office first thing tomorrow so that we can set the wheels in motion. You'll need your birth certificate or passport.'

'You looked it up?'

'Didn't you?'

'I'm in the wedding business, at least I hope

to be. I researched the subject thoroughly before I applied for a licence to use the chapel.'

'Of course you did. You always had a notebook with you. Lists… The big question is can you arrange a knock-your-socks-off wedding in four weeks?'

Knock…?

'I…' More throat clearing was required because this wouldn't be just any wedding. It would be *her* wedding. Miss Prideaux of Priddy Castle to Kamal Faulkner, the son of her grandparents' cook.

It was a great story.

If she played it for all it was worth she would get at least one of the lifestyle magazines interested. With a publicity shy multimillionaire as the groom, she could probably entice any one of them to run a feature.

It was going to have to be spectacular.

Style over substance.

'There will have to be an element of smoke and mirrors to hide the flaws,' she warned. 'A lot of fairy lights. The organ doesn't work so we'd need a string quartet. Enough flowers to fill a carnival float. All seen through a soft-focus lens.'

'I'll organise a local group to play for dancing, later,' he said. 'Let me know what you want for a first dance.'

Instantly a favourite song from her youth filled her head. She'd played it incessantly that summer, acting out her role as a teenage drama queen, until her grandfather had thrown her MP3 player into the creek and threatened to throw her after it.

Definitely not that one, no matter how appropriate the lyrics felt right now. The last thing she wanted to think about was him holding her, dancing to something romantic, something that they would have to practise.

'You're the musician. You decide.' Before he could offer any suggestions she said, 'I'll have enough to do organising the wedding. A fairground ride is always popular, maybe a butterfly release and charity donations instead of gifts.'

'Whatever you like,' he said. 'Just remember that it's not just a showcase for your business. It's your wedding.'

Her wedding?

'It's your wedding too,' she reminded him, just about keeping the sharpness out of her voice.

'Yes, of course. I didn't—'

'Is there anything you'd like?'

'Such as?'

'A whisky bar, clay-pigeon shooting for people who stay over and make a weekend of it. A treasure hunt. A river trip with a champagne picnic…'

'No shooting, but maybe a treasure hunt, and a river picnic trip sounds good.'

'I'll need a guest list from you.' Then, because she couldn't leave it any longer, 'I'm going to have to pay deposits, Kam, and I don't have any credit.'

'I'll sort that out first thing tomorrow.'

'Thank you.'

'This is a two-way partnership, Agnès. I don't need thanks. I'll meet you in the car park at nine o'clock tomorrow morning.'

They were going to arrange their wedding and, no matter what her concerns about his motives, he was giving her a great deal and she had to give him something back. Something meaningful.

'I'll be on the beach at seven. Meet me there. Without the dogs.' She didn't wait for him to ask why but ended the call.

A few moments later her phone pinged to let her know that she had a text message. It was his number. Nothing else.

For a while she sat with her tablet on her knee, staring into the fire, trying not to think how different this ending could have been.

She was right. She knew she was.

The fact that he'd accepted her decision so easily suggested that he had other options. Someone he was rushing up to London to see, perhaps. Someone to whom he was going to have to explain the situation.

And she'd just made it easy for him with her 'no sex' stipulation.

Would another woman accept the situation? Believe it was going to be a marriage in name only? Would she?

Her mind recoiled from the emotional pit that gaped before her at the very thought of him being close to another woman while he was with her.

This was an old-fashioned arranged marriage; it was all about property and inheritance. She had to forget romance and focus on what it would mean for everyone who worked at the castle. Her grandmother. The fact that it would preserve the estate from development.

She needed to concentrate on the list.

She'd attach the surveyor's report on the roof when she sent it to Kam. She was sure he had a good idea of the problems, but she was determined that he could never be able to say that she'd hidden the truth from him. Not about the castle, anyway.

Her emotions were her own business.

Maybe, having slept on it, he'd go straight to London in the morning and look for somewhere less troublesome for his city kids.

London?

Hold on…

She took out her phone and texted.

What were you thinking of doing with Henry while you're in London?

His reply was swift. Almost as if he'd been sitting there, waiting for her to catch up.

I wasn't sure how he'd be in a car so Suz offered to look after him.

Suz? He'd been talking to Suz?

She swallowed. Why wouldn't he? It was her job to take care of the needs of a guest. It was stupid to be hurt because he hadn't asked her. After the way she'd reacted, why would he?

She sent another text.

Just checking. I'll see you in the morning.

You do know that you don't have to stay over there on the island?

About to reply that she didn't 'have' to do anything, she stopped herself. That so wasn't true.

She had to marry him. Have his baby.

Why did you come over here? she texted.

Why did you?

Before she could even think of an answer that didn't betray her, he sent another message.

That's a rhetorical question, btw.

She frowned, confused. She was there to avoid him. Why would he want to avoid her?

No. Don't go there.

The list. Concentrate on the list.

Once she'd sent it to him she turned her thoughts to the wedding. Despite what he'd said, she had to forget that it was her wedding. It was going to be the showcase for the castle as a must-have wedding location and had to be perfect.

Burnt orange was the in colour this season. She would have to research roses to find the best colour—maybe Super Trouper or Sparkle. She'd set them against the sharp lime-green of *alchemilla mollis*. Orange ribbons for the pew ends. Bridesmaids?

Suzanna and some little girls whose families had a connection with the castle. She grinned. Jimmy, the heating engineer who had done so much for her boiler, had twin six-year-olds.

Ivory dresses with orange sashes because ivory was the colour of the dress her mother had worn. And her mother before her. And her mother before that. Soft ivory lace with a long lace veil held in place by the tiara from the Prideaux parure.

Fake diamonds for a fake wedding.

For a moment she thought it had begun to rain, then she realised that the drops on her screen were her tears.

For a moment she gave in to the pity tears, sitting in the dark with her arms wrapped tightly around herself, wishing Kam were there to hold her, reassure her, tell her that it would be all right.

That was never going to happen. If it was going to be all right, it would be because she made it so, and she wiped her cheeks with the palms of her hands and then made up the fire.

A moth danced close to the flames but was wafted away on the rising heat before it became toasted. In the distance a tawny owl began to make its long, ghost-like hoots and she crawled into the bivouac, snuggled up in Kam's sleeping bag and lay wrapped in his scent, listening to the tiny rustling of small creatures, until she fell asleep.

CHAPTER NINE

The registrar has been booked, the date set for Saturday the first of June. Jimmy's daughters and Pam and Sandra's granddaughters are going to be bridesmaids, I've booked a carousel, a butterfly release and the vintage steamer Queen of the Creek *for a lunch trip on the day after the wedding for those guests who are staying on. The editor of a celebrity gossip magazine offered to pay for the honeymoon if they could have an exclusive to cover the wedding. That is never going to happen. They'd send a photographer to follow us around, wanting intimate pictures of the two of us together. We compromised on photographs of preparations for the wedding ahead of the day in return for a sizable donation to charity.*

Agnès Prideaux's Journal

KAM WALKED DOWN to the beach just before seven. Agnès was already there, sitting on a rock, a decent-sized sea trout beside her.

'I hope you've got a licence for that,' he said.

'I have a licence that covers all castle guests.'

'And there was I, thinking I was reliving my bad-boy past.'

'We all have to grow up, Kam.'

'Do we? Children aren't constrained by the needs of adults. They are free to live in their imaginations. If I'd been a proper grown-up, I'd have been worried about paying the rent, the mortgage like Raj, just grateful to keep things on an even keel. I wouldn't have taken the risks I did.'

'I was stubborn,' she said, 'but I didn't take any risks. I didn't have your courage.'

'What would you have done differently?'

'Followed you. Hunted you down and made you listen to me.'

What? He was just staring at her like an idiot and she shook her head, turned away to pick up something on the rock beside her, which she tossed to him.

He caught it more by reflex than skill and

found himself holding an ancient leather gauntlet, the kind used by falconers. It was cracked with age, another attic find that Agnès had given him when he wanted to train an osprey he'd found with a broken wing and nursed back to health.

He'd left it behind on his bedroom floor, telling himself he'd wanted nothing of hers. A lie. He'd once been asked which of his possessions he'd grab in a fire and had instantly said it would be his guitar.

He'd had dreams of owning an electric guitar like his heroes in the posters that decorated his walls, but Agnès had gifted him a fine acoustic guitar that he fell in love with the moment he felt the silk of the wood beneath his fingers, touched the strings and heard a different kind of music.

She'd told him that she'd found it in an attic, that no one would miss it, but he'd seen the case propped up in a corner of the music room and a label on the inside of the case bore her father's name. It had been a gift of pure love from one child to another.

'What is this?' he asked, holding the glove.

'Ozzie was my only link with you.' She picked up the fish and offered it to him. 'Whistle and she'll come.'

'Ozzie?' He looked stunned. 'She's still alive?'

'Ospreys can live for twenty years,' she said. 'The river warden caught me fishing for her once but, when I told him it was for your osprey, he wrote me out a special permit that lasts for her lifetime.'

'What a sweet smile will get you,' he said, flippantly, turning away so that she would not see the emotion threatening to engulf him. While he had been filled with anger, she had been all about love, and at that moment all he wanted to do was hold her, tell her how much he'd missed her. How much he wished he'd come back sooner.

Instead he pulled on the gauntlet that had once been loose on his hand, but now fitted as snugly as if it had been made for him, took the fish and, holding it high above his head, he let out a long, low whistle.

For a moment there was nothing, but then he heard the thin, high answering call that dipped suddenly and then, with a rush of white breast, grey and black barred wings, she was there, talons reaching for the fish as she snatched it from his hand. As he took a step forward to watch her soar away with it, she dipped, turned and flew over him once and then again a second time as if to confirm that it was him, that he was back, before heading back up the creek to where he knew she would be raising her chicks.

Home.

Not just hers, but his. He wanted to whoop like a boy but when he turned to Agnès he saw that there were tears in her eyes and, still wearing the gauntlet, he put his arms around her, drawing her close enough to smell the rosemary in her shampoo.

They stood like that for a long time, just holding one another, his lips brushing her hair and every cell in his body urging him to go for broke and say the words. Just say the words…

He fought the impulse. She had no earthly reason to believe that he had, in the last few days, come to realise what should have been blindingly obvious; that it wasn't anger that had kept her at the forefront of his mind. Anger would have long been blown away by his success. To feel that much passion there had to be something far stronger, more powerful, unchanging.

One day she would know. He would work to show her in every way possible. But for now, she'd laid down the rules of engagement. He had accepted her terms and only she could change them.

'Hey,' he said, after a while when holding her without breaking down and kissing her was straining him to breaking point. 'I don't know about you, but I could do with some breakfast.'

The only answer was a little sniff.

Tears were good. They were an emotional valve and breakfast together would be a chance to become closer before their visit to the registrar. At least it would have been but Jamie was in the kitchen, leaning against the dresser, a mug of coffee in his hand.

'Guests normally eat in the breakfast room,' he growled.

Kam held his temper in the face of the man's rudeness.

'Agnès and I are getting married as soon as

it can be arranged,' he replied, determined to leave the chef in no doubt that whatever hope he had in her direction was history. 'I'm kitchen company.'

'Married, is it? So why's the lass got tears in her eyes?'

'Kam just had an emotional reunion with Ozzie,' Agnès said, before he could tell the man it was none of his business.

'If ye say so.' He poured the remains of his coffee down the sink and placed the mug in the dishwasher. 'I'm to m'work. Ye know where I'll be if ye need me, Agnès.'

'Jamie…' Agnès took a step after him, but he was gone.

'Your chef seems very at home in the castle. Does he have a room here?'

'What? Oh, no. He has a flat down on the quay. I imagine he came over to check with Suzanna about craft guest numbers this weekend. He uses this kitchen to prepare dishes that we can pop in the oven for them,' she added, responding to his raised eyebrows.

'Is that part of your contract with the caterers?' he asked. Having read it, he knew the answer.

'What do you think?'

'I think it sounds like another of your under-the-counter arrangements. Like the heating engineer,' he added when she looked blank.

'I…yes. Sounds like, I mean. It's not the same at all.'

'I realise you've been under financial pressure, Agnès, but once I'm involved everything has to be above board and accountable. Whatever private arrangements you have must stop right now. Private arrangements of any kind,' he added.

'He does it in his own time,' she protested. 'I provide the ingredients and he adds the magic.'

'For which you pay him.'

'Oh, I see. You're worried that he doesn't pay tax.' She shook her head. 'It isn't like that. He's a long way from home and I think he's lonely.'

'Lonely?'

'Suzanna was talking about a favourite dish from home that she was missing and he offered to try and cook it for her. It grew from there. I think he enjoys working in a kitchen where no one is telling him what he can or can't cook.'

'I don't think it's the kitchen that's the attraction.'

'Then what...? Oh...' She sat down rather suddenly. 'How could I have been so stupid?' The question wasn't addressed to him, but rather to herself. 'How on earth could I have missed...?' She shook her head, surprised, but apparently not horrified to discover the chef had feelings for her.

'If his company find out what he's doing he could lose the job he so desperately needs,' he said, sharply.

'That seems harsh.'

'You may not be paying him but you are selling the food he prepares. I think they would take the view that under the terms of their contract they should be being paid for that.'

'If they cooked food anyone wanted to eat, I'd gladly pay them,' she replied, clearly irritated. 'In the meantime, since you are now kitchen company, I'll leave you to help yourself to breakfast while I go and shower off the smell of fish.'

He sighed. They'd been on the point of turning a corner this morning. Instead they were having an argument about that damn chef and, since his appetite had deserted him, he filled a mug with coffee and then called his mother to tell the news.

'Do you have to inform anyone before I place an announcement in the broadsheets?' Kam asked, as they left the register office, later that morning.

Agnès shook her head.

'Not even Pierre Prideaux?'

'I have no doubt he's got someone keeping him informed about the situation at the castle. He'll know the minute the notice is posted and he'll be checking you out in the hopes of finding something that will give him cause to challenge the wedding. A wife in London, or a live-in lover with half a dozen children…?'

'I've been a bit busy for a secret life of any kind, Agnès. It would be a kindness to tell him not to waste his money.'

'What about your mother?'

'I called her this morning. She was happily

unsurprised. Asked me what had taken me so long.'

'Oh.'

'She sent you her love. She has classes booked in for the next couple of weeks but she'll call you and she'll be over in plenty of time for the wedding.'

'Did you explain—?'

'We don't have to explain ourselves to anyone but, since the registrar is watching us out of her office window, I do think it might be a good idea if I kiss you before I get in my car. You were so nervous I thought she was going to take you into her office and ask if you were being coerced.'

'I'm sorry. I thought it would be just a formality. Answer a few questions, sign a form, but the hugeness of it overcame me.'

'I'm glad you felt that way.' He raised his hand to cradle her cheek, long fingers tangling in her hair, resting against her temple as he looked down at her. 'It is a huge thing we're doing and it's only natural that you'd have reservations.'

'No…' Her heart was hammering in her chest and she forgot to breathe. 'No reservations.'

At least their first kiss wasn't to be in the street, with people walking past, just to convince the registrar, who had commented on her nervousness, that this was the real thing.

If the woman could see the way her legs were shaking, feel how her heart was pounding, the ache low down in her belly at the thought of even this very public kiss, she would have no doubt that this bride-to-be could not wait for her wedding night.

As her head was filled with images of how that night could be, Kam took her in the lightest embrace and brushed his lips against hers. It was no more than a touch, in much the same way as a lightning bolt was no more than a touch that left the earth scorched and smoking with heat. It lasted for three shatteringly brief heartbeats and as he drew back a soft, betraying moan escaped her.

For a split second nothing happened, then he hauled her close and this time his mouth came down on hers with the impact of a meteor strike. The world continued to spin around her, traffic passed, someone whistled but her entire world was concentrated in the mind-altering experience of his kiss.

Seconds, minutes. She had no notion of how long it had lasted, only that she didn't ever want it to stop.

But then she was clinging to him and he was looking down at her, eyebrow raised in a silent query, asking her if she was all right.

She nodded, speech utterly beyond her.

'Is there anything you would like me to bring you from London?' he asked. 'Apart from an engagement ring.'

A ring…?

'Would you prefer a diamond or a coloured stone?'

Perhaps it was as well she couldn't speak, Agnès thought, because, as if reading her mind, he said, 'Don't say you don't want or need one. That isn't going to happen.'

'No.' Her mouth shaped the word but nothing came out. She tried again. 'For your pride?'

'For my pleasure,' he said gently. 'You'll be wearing it for a long time, so think about what you would like.'

'I was going to wear my mother's ring.'

'No.'

'People would understand. I'm wearing her wedding dress.'

'You can wear whatever dress makes you happy, but you're not wearing an engagement ring, no matter how emotionally attached you are to your mother's memory, that was chosen by another man for another woman.' He took her hand, wrapping his finger around hers. 'It's not about pride, Agnès. I want you to have something precious that is entirely yours. You deserve that.'

No one had ever said that to her before. That she deserved something. That she was worth anything.

'If you're not careful I'll weep all over you again and you're wearing a very nice suit.'

'I have another one, although I might not have time to go back to my flat and change before my first meeting.'

'And I'm delaying you.'

'You could come with me.'

She hesitated for just a moment. Wanting to be with him, see where he lived, ask him where he was going, who he was going to see, but then she shook her head. 'I could, but unfortunately dream weddings don't arrange themselves. It's going to take every spare minute of my time to organise everything.'

'About that. You asked me if there was anything I wanted.'

'Yes?'

'Don't turn it into an advertising feature for the castle, Agnès. Forget the media, the business. What I want is for you to give yourself the dream wedding you'd want if there was no one to see it but the people you love.'

'I've never had that dream.'

'It's never too late to dream,' he said, 'and that includes your ring. At least give me somewhere to start.'

'Something simple. A diamond will go with everything. And nothing too big or fancy or I'll have to take it off when I'm working.'

'A practical engagement ring for a very practical woman.' He was shaking his head but smiling, if a little wryly. 'I will do my best.'

'And could you pick up the parure for me?' She took the receipt from her pocket and handed it to him. 'People will expect me to wear the tiara and earrings. No one will know it's fake except us and the auction house and they won't tell.'

'I'll see to it. A courier will arrive with credit cards for you some time this morning. Pay Bridges' account, get your friendly heating engineer over to sort out the boiler and pay whatever it takes to get the roof and guttering repaired before the wedding. The interior will wait until we're away.' He glanced at his watch. 'I really do have to go. I have an appointment that won't keep.'

'Kam…' He waited. 'How long will you be gone?'

'A week, ten days, maybe.' He was still holding her hand and he raised it to his lips, brushing his lips across her knuckles. 'Take care of Henry for me.'

He let go of her hand, stepped into his car without a backward glance and in a second was lost in the stream of traffic.

'Drive safely,' she whispered, raising her hand to her face to catch the last scent of him. 'Come back soon.'

* * *

Kam had been gone a week but he'd texted her often, sent her a dozen photographs of rings, each one more wildly over the top, footballers' wives flashy than the one before.

He knew what she liked, simple things like the bracelet she was wearing now and she trusted him to find something that was just right. In the meantime it was fun to be teased a little.

Today's text wasn't fun, though.

I had hoped to be back this weekend but something's come up and I have to go away for a few days. Can you cope with Henry for a bit longer?

She'd replied.

I'll have to cope with Henry on a permanent basis. Where are you?

On board a plane and about to take off. I'll explain when I see you. If you need anything, call my office and talk to Michael.

He'd added a number.

Where are you going?

But she'd got no answer and was halfway through tapping in Michael's number to ask him where Kam had gone when she stopped.

She wasn't about to admit to anyone that he hadn't told her himself.

The bluebell woods were pulling in the visitors to the gardens, but when she went to the Orangery for a word with Jamie, he was gloomier than usual.

'What's up?'

'The repairs to the castle roof mean that the Orangery will be closing at the end of the week. Health and safety issues. I've just had a call from head office to say that they won't be reopening.'

'Won't...?'

'They're saying it hasn't made the kind of returns they'd expected and they're writing it off. I'd have thought they would have been in touch with you about that.'

'No doubt they've written to my lawyers,' she said. 'What about your job?'

'They've offered me one in Luton, but I'm staying here.'

'Good, because now you're free, you can cater the wedding for me.'

'I'm not sure your man will be happy with that.'

'My man has told me to do what I like, so start working on ideas for the menu. I'll let you know about special dietary requirements once I've had replies to the invitations. Oh, and, Jamie…' She smiled. 'Start planning on how we're going to run the new Orangery when we've got rid of all that orange plastic. Morning coffee with freshly made cookies and cakes, fabulous lunches and destination afternoon teas.'

'Agnès …'

'I'll want a champagne afternoon tea on the day before the wedding for the guests who will be staying over and the press who will be here to take photographs.'

He'd grabbed a notebook and was already scribbling down ideas.

'A fabulous lunch after the wedding. An evening buffet and then perhaps a couple of hot dishes to serve later, risotto, pasta…' she said, ticking the list off on her fingers. 'A buffet breakfast and then individual picnic hampers for the lunchtime river trip. Suz will co-ordinate numbers, dietary requirements, et cetera.'

As the days passed, the noise and mess were everywhere, there was no word from Kam, but at least the wedding plans were coming together.

There was just one problem.

The dress.

'It's hopeless, Agnès.' Lily was a skilled needlewoman who'd made wedding dresses for both her daughters and several nieces. She'd offered to help refit the dress Agnès's mother had worn but she was shaking her head. 'Women were a different shape when this were made, and your mother was a lot shorter than you.'

'I never realised,' she said.

'What you need is a modern interpretation of the dress.'

'I don't have time to have one made.'

'If you get a ready-to-wear dress, something simple, strapless, with a little train, I could use the lace from your mother's dress to make you a twenties-style overdress to cover your shoulders, just sliding off your arms. An open V to the waist, dropping in layers to somewhere around your knees. I saw something when I was making Lucy's dress…' She flicked through her phone, looking at photographs on a website. 'Like this.'

'Oh, my goodness,' Suz said. 'That is gorgeous. Can you really do that, Lily?'

She just grinned. 'Let's go shopping.'

There were no guests so the next morning Suz, Lily and Agnès caught the early train to London and returned, exhausted but giggly happy and laden with parcels, that evening to find Kam's car parked by the front door.

Lily whisked the dress off to the sewing room, Suz said she had to go to her room and change her shoes, leaving Agnès, heart in her mouth, to go and find Kam.

She hadn't reached the kitchen when there was an ear-piercing shriek from Suz's room.

She turned and went racing up the stairs, not sure what to expect, and found Suz embracing a girl who had to be her sister. Both of them were locked in the arms of a tall, slender woman who was the image of Suz.

She looked up, eyes filled with tears. 'I don't believe it. My mother and my sister…'

Kam. That was where he'd been…

Agnès turned to see him standing in the doorway and her first instinct was to fling herself at him and kiss him. She hesitated, fatally, trying to read him and then, as she took a step towards him, he said, 'Where were you?'

His question, the edge in his voice, stopped her in her tracks leaving her torn between regret at her lack of courage to just go for it the way that the teenage girl she had once been had gone for it, no holds barred, and crushing disappointment that he hadn't just stepped forward and swept her into his arms.

Clearly she'd misread that bone-melting kiss. Had it, after all, been for the registrar or had she disappointed him…?

Whatever, she wasn't going to apologise for not sitting at home waiting for him to return.

'If you'd called,' she said, 'or texted…'

'I assumed you would be completely occupied with the renovations to the castle, the wedding arrangements. It never occurred to me that you wouldn't be here.'

'Today is the first time I've been anywhere since you left,' she replied, barely able to stop herself from snapping.

She'd spent every minute while he'd been away chasing builders, plumbers, carpenters to make sure everything would be ready on time. Glued to the phone until her ear was red-hot as she organised her 'dream wedding'.

After a kiss that had blown away so many of her doubts, his urging to create a wedding for herself rather than the media, she had begun to believe in it, choosing things for herself, rather than for style.

Gone was the sophisticated burnt orange and lime green colour scheme. The chapel was to be filled with masses of wild foxgloves and cow parsley, the pew ends decorated with ribbons and roses from the garden. There was going to be a picnic in the grounds of the castle rather than a formal wedding breakfast, a million fairy lights, silent fireworks that wouldn't frighten the animals…

And then she thought about Kam. How he

must have felt when he arrived back, clearly exhausted, with this wonderful gift and it had fallen flat.

'I'm really sorry that we weren't here when you arrived, Kam. I had a bit of a dress drama.'

'I thought the dress was the one thing you had sorted.'

'I thought so, too, but I hadn't taken into account the fact that I'm a lot taller than my mother. What should have reached my ankles stopped halfway up my calves.'

'I'm sorry,' he said.

'It's sorted.'

He shook his head, dragged a hand through hair that was still damp from the shower. 'No. I'm sorry I was so sharp. Sorry I left you to deal with everything.'

She smiled. 'I'm not. What you've done is far more important.' While she'd been dreaming, he'd been moving mountains. 'Thank you…' Her breath caught in her throat. 'Just…thank you.' She dashed away a tear. 'Dammit, you are always making me cry.'

'As long as they are always tears of happiness,' he said, gravely, then held out a hand. 'We aren't needed here and I want to breathe some fresh creek air.'

'You need to sleep.'

'Later,' he said.

She took his hand and held it for a moment, trying to put everything she was feeling into that small contact.

'When did you get back?'

'Early this morning, but there were formalities to be gone through. A ton of paperwork. We arrived here about an hour ago. Maryam and Hani were understandably upset when Suz wasn't here. Pam thought it would be a good idea to take them up to her room so that they could be reassured by seeing her things. Sandra, bless her, made them mint tea and did her best to make them feel welcome.' His grip tightened on her hand. 'You have good people here.'

'I am unbelievably lucky to have found them.'

'As they are you.'

She gave an awkward little shrug. 'I'm guessing you didn't tell me where you were going in case it didn't happen.'

'There's always the possibility that things will go wrong at the last moment. Some family member or local official with a bee in his bonnet.'

'Is Suzanna's mother able to stay? I'm surprised her husband let her leave.'

'Her husband died a few months ago. Pneumonia at a guess. If I'd left her behind she would have had to rely on his brothers to take care of her. And Hani needs her mother.'

'How much did you have to pay to let them both go?'

He gave her a wry smile. 'That's a very unattractive cynical streak you have there, Miss Prideaux.'

'It's a very hard world, Mr Faulkner. How much?'

'Not much by First World standards,' he said. 'Nowhere near enough for such joy.'

'Not just for them,' she said. 'Nothing you could have done would have made me happier.'

'Even saving the castle from Pierre Prideaux?' When she didn't answer, he said, 'We're going to be married, have a child together, Agnès. I have to know what happened.'

'I know. And I will tell you,' she promised, 'but right now I want to hear how you became involved in rescuing Suz's sister.'

'Before the wedding,' he insisted, looking at her for a moment to impress on her that this was only a pause in that conversation.

She nodded and, apparently satisfied, he said, 'Suz broke down that evening you spent on the island and spilled it all out.'

'Just like that?' Suz was very careful who she talked to. People weren't always as supportive as you'd hope. 'Jamie knows her story. Lily and Sandra helped me take care of Suz after I found her half dead on the beach, but they don't talk about it.'

Kam called Dora and Henry. They came bounding out of her office and out of the door, circling them excitedly before racing away along the path to the creek, so it was a moment before he said, 'She caught me in your office looking for the catering contract.'

'Oh?'

'I explained that I was trying to help. She wasn't a pushover but eventually she gave me the contract to copy. I remembered you telling me about her sister and asked how it was going. The next minute she was weeping all over me.'

'You do seem to have that effect on women.'

'I'm working on getting them to smile,' he said. 'How am I doing?'

She laughed, shook her head. 'Whatever you're doing, keep doing it.' The path narrowed, and it was either walk single file or walk closer. She chose closer and, slipping her hand under his arm, said, 'Tell me more.'

'She'd had a call from her mother. It seems her uncle had accepted a dowry for Hani. Time was running out, but you had so many worries that she didn't want to burden you.'

Her legs were brushing against his thighs, her arm was pressed against his ribs so that she could feel his heart thumping and her body was drumming out *this*, *this*, *this* with every step.

If she stopped, turned to him so that her breasts were touching his sweater, her body pressed against his, would he kiss her again? What on earth had possessed her to impose a 'no sex' rule?

'I don't understand how you could fix things

so quickly,' she said. 'I've spent months dealing with people whose job involves pushing paper around in a circle until it falls down a hole.'

His shrug sent a current of awareness rippling through her and she stumbled like an idiot.

'I did the Foreign Secretary a favour when I was in India last year, so I gave him a call.'

At that she did stop but not to hurl herself at him. 'You did the Foreign Secretary a favour? *The Foreign Secretary?* What favour?'

'I could tell you, but then I'd have to kill you,' he said, brushing off her curiosity with a joke, but clearly it had been something sensitive and she didn't push it. 'He spoke to diplomats on the ground, who said they would handle it, but it was no longer just about paperwork. There would be compensation to be paid to her uncle or the man who wanted a ten-year-old wife. I wanted to be sure nothing went wrong.'

'And did it? Go wrong?'

'Nothing that I couldn't handle.' He glanced at her as they moved on. 'Did you get everything you wanted today?'

'Everything and considerably more. Suz and Pam are a bad influence.'

'As long as you enjoyed yourself.'

'You may not say that when you see how much I've spent since you've been away.'

'Money means nothing unless it's serving a useful purpose.'

'I'm not sure wedding shoes can be described as useful.'

'On the contrary. They will carry you down the aisle to me. I can't think of anything more useful than that. How are things going with that? Are you sticking to the dream?'

'I had a little hiccup' she confessed, 'but Lily, and a pair of pink shoes, straightened me out.'

'Pink shoes?'

'With peep toes and bows. They might not be traditional but I'm afraid it was love at first sight. I changed my entire colour scheme to fit around them.'

'Lucky shoes,' he said.

They'd reached the beach.

Kam had changed into trainers and jeans after his shower but Agnès, still in city shoes, paused to step out of them and he watched as she put them on a rock out of harm's way before joining him on the sand.

She'd fallen in love with a pair of shoes? Built her wedding around them?

He'd been living on the memory of a kiss, believing that things had moved on, imagined Agnès throwing herself into his arms as he returned with Suz's family.

Maybe if he hadn't been left to stew in impatience for an hour he wouldn't have hesitated to sweep her up into her arms and give her the kiss he'd been dreaming about. But he'd seen her hesitation…

They crossed to a fallen tree, silvered with age and worn smooth by people using it as a seat.

'I love this spot,' Kam said, letting the silence seep into his bones along with a dozen scents and sounds that were part of the creek. Wet sand, the hint of ozone drifting up the creek from the ocean beyond, the clank of rigging against yachts, the chitter of a tern.

Even at six years old Agnès had known how

to sit quietly and just listen until the soft buzz of the woods, the creek resolved into individual sounds so that you could pick out each bird call, the scuffle of squirrels as they leapt through the trees, the stealthy swish of a fox moving through the undergrowth.

'The trees on the island need attention,' she said.

'It'll be a project I can work on with the youngsters who come here,' he said. 'They won't be able to resist the chance of being let loose with a chainsaw.'

'You're going to hand them chainsaws?'

He grinned, reached for her hand, loving that he could still catch her out, and without warning she was blushing, flustered as the little girl who'd been caught trailing after him.

How had he not realised that he loved her? Wasting time in London, in India, anywhere but here.

The kiss he'd stolen after their visit to the registrar had left him weak with longing. He'd pulled over into a layby as soon as he was clear of the town, not trusting himself on the motorway until he'd stopped shaking.

'I owed you that one,' he said, then, suddenly aware that the beach was empty, 'Where are the dogs?'

CHAPTER TEN

Wedding plans are proceeding. Not quite as I had imagined, but Kam is home with Suzanna's family and all should be smooth sailing, but there are always last-minute hiccups, bruised egos and some very real bruises.

Agnès Prideaux's Journal

KAM STOOD UP, called Henry and the dog poked his head up over the dinghy's hull.

'He's in the boat.' He turned back and grinned at her. 'How did you manage that?'

'Since their first encounter Henry has fallen under Dora's spell. He follows her everywhere. And Dora loves nothing better than to be rowed across the creek. I hoped that when he saw her jump in, he might follow.'

'It was that easy?'

'No, Kam. I had to do it every day for a week

before Henry cracked and followed her. He whined pitifully the first time but she lay beside him and now he's fine. You can stay on the island whenever you like now.'

'The island?'

'You're welcome,' she said.

'I'm sorry, that deserves a kiss.'

'That would be nice.' She angled her head to meet it, closing her eyes, her mouth fluttering like a nervous butterfly as his lips touched her, desperately hoping that this was going to be it, the kiss that would make the years disappear. Make the future a possibility. Instead he cradled her head in her hands and kissed her forehead as if she were his sister.

Which answered any question she cared to ask about the kiss outside the register office. He'd been putting on a show. And what a show it had been. She had been totally convinced.

Forget the turkey-baster baby. She didn't have a lot of experience to go on but she could recognise a turkey-baster kiss when it was at home.

'Do you want to walk along to the quay?' Kam asked. 'We could call in at the Ferryside and you can tell me everything that's been happening. Maybe have something to eat?'

'I need to get back,' she said, standing up and taking a step in the direction of the rock where she had left her shoes, needing to put some distance between them. 'I have to sort out somewhere for Maryam and Hani to sleep.'

Sort out what was going on in her head.

'Can't Sandra…?' His moment of frustration was quickly controlled. 'I'm sorry, of course you'll want to do that yourself.'

'Are you coming?' she asked.

'I need to walk off the flight. Or maybe I'll just take Henry for a trip around the island. If you can spare Dora?'

'Just try and leave her behind.'

'They are an improbable pair.'

There was, she thought, a lot of it about.

'If you need something to eat, Jamie is catering the wedding and has taken up more or less permanent residence in the kitchen.'

'He's still here? Didn't the catering company offer him another job?' His poker face failed him for once. He was not happy.

'Was that part of the deal?' she asked.

'Deal?'

'I imagine I have you to thank for the fact that they decided to pull out of the Orangery contract.'

He shrugged. 'I offered them a choice. An audit of their books or the chance to walk away with the profits.' He said it as if it were nothing. 'I knew you were concerned about Jamie, so I added a job for him to the agreement.'

'They stuck to the terms of your deal, but he didn't want to leave Castle Creek and I've asked him to take over the running of the Orangery when it reopens.'

He made no comment, just walked across to the boat before, as if it were an afterthought, saying, 'If you have time, I'd like a tour of the works in the morning. Is nine too early?'

'Nine will be perfect. I have a meeting in the chapel at eight-thirty. You'll find me there.'

She didn't wait for an answer but brushed the sand from her feet, slipped on her shoes and walked quickly back to the castle. She'd rowed her hands raw to get his stupid dog to sit in a boat and he'd kissed her forehead!

And what on earth was his problem with

Jamie? They had clashed that first day, but he'd said nothing Kam hadn't deserved. The man was a sweetheart and she was lucky to have him.

As for her dream wedding, the one built on a single kiss, she should have stuck with her original plan. Style over substance, like the marriage it was meant to celebrate.

Tomorrow. They would talk tomorrow.

Tonight she had to put on a happy face for Maryram and Hani and Suz and eat the dish that Jamie had cooked especially for them. The evening was a joyful one, filled with both tears and laughter, but for her it was a bittersweet occasion.

This happiness had been given to them by Kam and he should have been there to celebrate with them.

Kam waited until she was out of sight, watching the swing of her long dark hair, her long legs. She was holding her head up high but he would have given anything to see her expression. To know what she was feeling.

He waited until she was out of sight before

lifting his hand to his mouth as if to preserve the tingle where he'd kissed her. Had he imagined that she was trembling? Or had that been his own struggle to hold back?

He'd totally lost it that day outside the register office. He had intended no more than a touch of lips to convince the wretched woman that he wasn't forcing Agnès to marry him against her will. As if anyone could force her to do anything.

But the little moan that escaped her lips had snapped his careful restraint and she had fully participated in the kiss that followed. He'd hoped it was a turning point but had she thought it was just part of the show?

She'd hadn't wanted to wear his ring and tonight she'd raised her lips to him as if it was a duty.

He didn't want duty; she had to show him if she wanted more from him, that she might, after all, return his feelings.

Right now, it seemed as if it was the pugnacious and protective chef she couldn't let go, even when she was sacrificing herself on the altar of the damned castle.

Right at the moment, he could have taken a match to it himself.

Henry gave an impatient bark, standing up in the boat, urging him to come on board, but Dora leapt out and trotted over to lean against his ankle as if she understood.

'Not so silly, are you?' he said, scooping her up. She licked his neck, then nestled herself in the crook of his arm, like a little warm comfort blanket. 'Am I being an idiot?'

The answer, since he was asking a dog for advice, was plainly yes and it didn't get any better. Having found no answers in the long walk along the creek path to the quay, he went into the bar of the Ferryside to slake his thirst first with a beer, and then numb his feelings with a large Scotch.

He knew there was no solution to be found in the bottom of a glass but he was in no hurry to go back to the castle. Henry, however, had other ideas. After an hour, he stood and growled quietly at his side until the landlord gently suggested he take his dog's advice and go home.

There was the faint scent of something spicy

in the kitchen; no doubt the sainted Jamie had cooked Suz's favourite dish for her family. He might wish the man to Hades, but his stomach was growling and, having settled the dogs in the mud room, he raided the fridge for leftovers.

Agnès, he decided, had a point. Even cold, it was the best thing he'd eaten in a week.

He knew he was behaving like a jealous oaf, for no good reason. She might not be in love with him but Agnès wouldn't cheat. With luck she'd put his behaviour down to exhaustion. Or he could just tell her the truth. That leaving her standing on the side of the road outside the registrar's office with the taste of her mouth on his lips had just about torn his heart out.

Maybe it was as simple telling her that he loved her.

Smiling to himself, he unhooked his key from its place behind the reception desk and made his way up to the Captain's Suite.

He'd just slid it into the lock when he heard a tap on a door out of sight, around the corner. No doubt Suz and her family still finding things to talk about. He turned the key, opened the door then stopped as he heard a man's voice, then a soft laugh from Agnès …

There was only one man around here with an accent like that. The pair of them were in her room and in a blind rage he strode down the corridor to see Agnès with her arms around Jamie.

He was already swinging his fist when he saw a movement in the room behind them.

Suzanne?

Confused, he hesitated and the next moment found himself flat on the floor, looking up at Agnès. She was standing over him, hands on hips, glaring at him with an expression that had pretty much the same power to sober him up as Jamie's fist.

'What on earth do you think you're doing?'

'Making a fool of myself?' he suggested, hoping that she might smile.

He felt as if he'd been hit by a half-brick but still had enough sense to realise that it was Suzanna fussing over Jamie, kissing his knuckles, putting her arm around him, doing the *there,*

there bit that if he wasn't such an idiot Agnès would be doing for him.

'I love you,' he said, because right at that moment nothing less would do.

'Have you been drinking?'

Her hair was loose around her face, she'd taken off every scrap of make-up and was wearing something loose and baggy with a cartoon mouse on the front that didn't quite make it to her knees.

'Not enough, because I'm stone-cold sober.'

'Sober as a newt. Jamie, help me to get him up.'

Jamie looked as if he was ready to help him over the tower battlements.

'I can manage,' he said quickly and made it to his feet unaided, despite the fact that his head was still swimming from the blow. He eased his jaw, gingerly testing to make sure it was all in one piece.

'Okay, drama over,' Agnès said. 'Suzanna, you'd better put some ice on Jamie's hand.'

'Y-yes…'

'You,' she said, taking his elbow in an iron grip, 'will come with me.'

'It's Jamie and Suzanna?' he said, as she frog-marched him back to his suite. 'But you were hugging him.'

'Because they came to tell me, wanted me to be the first to know, that they're engaged to be married.'

He let slip an expletive. 'Sorry…'

She stopped at his door. 'You asked me if there was anyone, Kam. Do you honestly think I would take everything that you are offering and then…?' Words apparently failed her. 'Does that hurt?'

'Not much,' he lied. Nowhere near as much as he deserved.

'That's a pity. Do you need to go to A & E?'

'No,' he said, trying not to wince as she ran soft, cool fingers lightly over his jaw, checking to make sure. 'I'm sorry. I'll apologise to Jamie and Suzanna in the morning, but I don't know what I can ever say—'

'Don't!' She held up a warning finger. 'Not another word. Go and sit down before you fall down while I fetch something to put on that.'

He knew that voice. His mother had used exactly that tone when he'd fallen out of a tree and his new jacket had been torn and covered in blood. As a boy he'd thought it was anger at the damage to his clothes. Having lived a little longer, seen a lot more, he knew that the anger was driven by fear of how much worse it could have been. By love.

He had yet to discover how much worse this was going to be. Whether he could ever put it right. Agnès's anger was the only thing that gave him hope.

Suzanna had Jamie's hand in a bowl of crushed ice by the time Agnès made it to the kitchen.

'I'm so sorry, Jamie.'

'No worries,' he said, grinning. 'I thought he was a cold fish, that you were making a mistake, Agnès, but you've got to like a guy who'll go in fighting for his lassie.'

'He just lay there on the floor and said he loved you,' Suzanna said, with a sigh. 'That's so romantic.'

It was barbaric, she thought, but he had shown his feelings in the clearest way possible. And he'd said the only words that mattered, not in some clichéd *I love you* moment when she wouldn't have known whether he meant it or was just saying what he thought she wanted to hear.

That declaration had had an undeniable ring of truth.

She gave both Suzanna and Jamie a hug. 'Name the day and your wedding will be my—our—gift to you both.'

'Hold that.'

Kam was lying propped up on the bed, only half awake, when something hard and wet was slapped against his jaw.

'Agnès —'

'Take these.'

He gritted his teeth and took bag of frozen peas and the painkillers she offered, washing the pills down with the bottle of water she handed him.

'He was in your room,' he said, as she turned away, desperate for her to understand how that had made him feel. 'You had your arms around him.'

'Tomorrow, Kam. We'll talk about this tomorrow.'

'Please… Just let me say this.' He shook his head, wished he hadn't, but this wasn't the moment to let a thumping headache get in the way of what he had to say. Because if ever there was a moment for honesty, openness, this was it. 'I'm sorry. I'm sorry I got it so wrong—'

'I don't understand how you could even think I'd do that.'

'Because I was being vile to you,' he said. 'He was being protective, standing up for you. I refused to admit it then, but that was the moment that I knew…'

'What? What did you know, Kam?'

'It was the moment that I knew why I'd come back. I thought it was all about showing everyone that they were wrong about me but today, coming across the creek on the ferry, knowing that you'd be there, waiting for me, the sun was shining.'

'It's rained nearly all day,' she pointed out.

'It was a metaphorical sun.'

'Oh.' She looked down so that he shouldn't see that she was trying not to smile.

'It was raining the day I left,' he said, 'and it has been raining ever since. That's metaphorical rain,' he added, hoping to make her laugh, but when she looked up there was no trace of the smile.

She was marrying him because she felt he deserved his legacy, but he didn't want a convenient marriage, he wanted a real one; he wanted her in his arms, in his life, in his bed.

'It was raining the day I came back,' he said, going for broke, 'but it's been getting brighter, warmer each day and today I knew that I was coming home and if it had been throwing down thunder, lightning and hail, the sun would still have been shining for me.'

'Metaphorically.'

'I'm not making much sense, am I?'

'Home?' she prompted.

'Not to Priddy Castle, Agnès. I thought it mattered, that taking it would put everything right, but we can't go back, we can't change what happened. We can only go on and live better lives. That's what I've discovered since I came back. That I wanted to stay here and make a good life with you. I just didn't know how to tell you.'

'You're telling me now,' she said, sitting on the bed beside him.

'Clearly it took Jamie to knock some sense into me.'

'You said you loved me. Did you mean it?'

'I was prepared to do anything to prove that to you.' He tossed the peas aside and took her hand. 'Save the castle. Help Suzanna's family, even have a damn turkey-baster baby if that's what it took to win you back…'

'No.'

The word hit him as hard as Jamie's fist. He physically recoiled, groaned. 'I've done it again,' he said, wanting to draw her into his arms and hold her, but unsure how she would react. 'I've made you cry.'

'Is that why the world's gone blurry?' Her voice was thick with emotion, but her fingers closed around his hand, holding him close. 'I was afraid, Kam. Afraid that you would take what you wanted, get your heir and then leave me. That would have been your perfect revenge.'

'You thought I could do that?' Even as he said it, he could see why she might believe it.

'It would have given you everything.'

'Everything I thought I wanted. Nothing of any worth. Revenge is a wild justice, Agnès. You lose a lot more than you think you've gained.'

'You say that and yet you thought I could take everything you were offering and still cheat on you with Jamie.'

'My heart said no, but everywhere I turned he was there and you were standing up for him.'

'I didn't realise… I knew you didn't like him but I thought your problem with him was all about that first day when he challenged you.'

'It didn't help. It's a long time since anyone did that. Except you. But then you always did.'

'You can never say that you didn't know what you were getting.'

'I'm not your grandfather. I want an equal as a wife, a woman who will stand toe to toe with me when she has to, by my side always. I should have told you how I felt when I asked you to marry me, but I thought, after the way I behaved when I arrived, that you'd think I was just saying what I thought you wanted to hear.'

'Instead you acted.'

'I wanted to show you—'

'I'm not talking about the castle, or about Suzanna's family. I'm talking about when you tried to hit Jamie.' Her eyes were sparkling through the tears. *'In vino veritas.'*

'I would have hit him if Suzanna hadn't distracted me. And for the record I would have done the same if I'd been stone-cold sober. But you're right about him. He is a damn fine chef.'

'Tell him that and he'll forgive you anything.'

'The only person I care about forgiving me is you. If I could go back to the day I arrived and do things differently…'

'What would you do, Kam?'

'Stand in your office doorway and watch you for a while and then, when you looked around, I'd smile and say I've missed you. Because that's the honest truth. Whenever something unusual caught my eye my first thought was *Agnès will love this*... It was infuriating, but it was so much a part of who I was that I couldn't stop myself.'

She laid a hand against his face. 'Do you think I don't know? A dolphin swam up the creek last summer and I actually turned to call you.'

He wiped his fingers across her wet cheeks

then across his own, anointing himself with her tears in a primeval gesture that bound them together as no vow ever could.

'I love you, Agnès Prideaux. I always have, always will.' He stood up and she put out a hand to steady him as the room swung.

'Are you all right, Kam?'

'Never better,' he said, and then he went down on his knees and, taking her hand in his, he said, 'Ignore everything we have said until this moment, wipe the slate clean. I love you, Agnès Prideaux. Will you honour me by becoming my wife?'

Kam Faulkner was the proudest man that Agnès had ever known and he was on his knees in front of her but, like him, she wanted an equal partnership and she sank to her knees in front of him.

'On the first of June, I will be in the chapel waiting for you and I will give you my whole heart. No reservations. No limits.' And then she took his face in both hands and kissed him.

The heartbeat before his lips answered hers felt like an eternity, as if the world were holding its breath, then he gathered her in, kissing her with a tender sweetness that melted all lingering doubts.

The warmth, his scent, was so familiar that it felt like coming home; thrilling, and yet at the same time it was so new that she shivered.

He drew back a little, asking the silent question. Did she want this? Had he misread the moment? Beyond words, she uttered a shameless little moan. She had waited a lifetime for this moment and she reached up, tangling her fingers in Kam's hair, drawing him back to her, deepening the kiss.

They were so close that she could feel his heart pounding next to hers as the silk of his tongue claimed her mouth, lighting up the long smouldering touchpaper of desire, and for a moment everything was perfect.

After a while he drew back a little.

'I have something for you. I was going to give it to you on the beach but now I'm glad I totally messed that up because this is the perfect moment.' He reached into his pocket and produced a small velvet box. 'I listened to everything you said, and I described what you wanted to a jewellery designer who came highly recommended. This is what she created for you.'

Agnès held her breath as Kam opened the box, but there, nestling against pale blue velvet, was the ring she would have designed for herself. A simple, plain band of white gold into which three large diamonds had been flush set. They caught the lamplight and flashed back a rainbow of colours.

'It's apparently called a gypsy setting,' Kam said, lifting it out. 'The diamonds don't sparkle as much as in other settings, but it's hard-wearing and easy to clean.' Then, clearly realising that wasn't quite how it was meant to be, he said, 'That came out all wrong.'

She would have laughed, but as she looked up she saw uncertainty in his eyes, the hunted look of a man who had tried to do something wonderful but found the result ashes in his hands.

'No.' She shook her head. 'It came out exactly right. It's absolutely perfect.'

'You're not just saying that? Maybe you'd like to talk to her yourself.'

'It's as if you read my mind and then created something way beyond my imagination.' He still looked doubtful and she held out her hand. 'Will you put it on? To make sure it fits?'

Of course it fitted. She wiggled her fingers and the diamonds sparkled back at her.

'I love it.' She looked up. 'I love you.'

He swayed slightly and she suddenly realised how grey he looked.

'Kam?'

'I'm just tired.'

'I'll stay with you.'

'No.' He took her hand. 'Not here. Not in this room.' He heaved himself to his feet, sat on the bed and lay back. 'We have a date, you and I… The first of June…'

He was asleep before his head hit the pillow.

She loosened his belt, eased off his trousers and covered him with the blanket then, unsure whether he was exhausted or suffering from the effects of the blow to his chin, she curled up on the bed beside him and watched him until his colour returned. Only leaving when the sky began to grow light in the east.

'Let's leave it at that, Agnès.' The door to the chapel had opened and she didn't need to look around to know that it was Kam. The flower arranger's indulgent smile warned her long before he came up behind her and she felt the weight of his arm across her shoulders.

'Hello, Mrs George. How's Harry?'

'He's well, thank you, Kam. Looking forward to the wedding.'

Neither of them spoke until the door closed behind her, the only movement that of the dust motes dancing in the shafts of coloured light streaming in through the stained glass.

Kam broke the silence. 'I've made my peace with Jamie about last night, Apologised to Suzanna.'

'I have a question about that.'

'Only one?'

'I was wondering how you knew that room was mine.' She turned to look up at him.

'It was years ago. I wanted to see where you lived. How you lived. Your grandfather had gone to London, you were away at school and I slipped in through the back door and walked through every room. Your room was so bare, it had fewer comforts than mine. I only knew it was yours because of the books you had, and the pictures drawn by your mother hanging on the wall.'

'Did you feel sorry for me?'

'Not sorry for you. Sad for you.'

'There was a teddy bear on my pillow when I came home one holidays. It smelled faintly of woodsmoke. You didn't say anything but I knew it had to be yours. I still have it.' She put her hand in his. 'Come and sit down. I need to tell you something.'

'Is this going to be bad?'

'It's family business and you are going to be my family.'

She'd never told the story to anyone before and it took her a moment to organise her thoughts. 'This,' she said, with a gesture that took in the chapel, 'the sweet legend on the website about how Henri Prideaux fell in love with the young Elizabeth Draycott, is all lies. Henri Prideaux, dashing smuggler, hero of a dozen fanciful stories, was a monster.'

That was clearly not what Kam was expecting. An eyebrow rose, but he waited.

'Elizabeth was just sixteen years old when he raped her.' Her voice wobbled as she thought of herself, only a few weeks younger, eager, full of anticipation, wanting to give herself to the boy she adored; how different, how terrifying, how painful it must have been for Elizabeth. 'Shame, fear, kept her silent. When it became obvious that she was pregnant, Henri swore to her father, in this chapel, on the family bible that still sits on that lectern, that she'd thrown herself at him. He acted out the role of a decent man, tormented beyond his strength, but said he'd save her from the shame and marry her. She was not given a choice. Within weeks of their son being born, her father fell from the tower.'

'Murder?'

'When Elizabeth suggested it had not been an accident Henri warned her that she and her infant son would go the same way, if she didn't behave. And, should she have any ideas of her own in that direction, his son by his first wife would take his place and he would see that she and her precious boy followed him to Hades.'

'Like father like son?'

'Elizabeth had no one to fight for her so she buckled under, did her duty and bore him seven children before, mercifully, he fell in the creek after drinking one too many bottles of the brandy in his cellar. His French son arrived, as promised, no doubt planning to take possession, but Elizabeth had wasted no time in summoning the local militia to guard her children and the lawyers had a will written in Henri's own hand and sealed with his ring.'

'With the entail.'

'With the entail,' she agreed. 'There was only one problem with that. Unlike his wife Henri could not read or write English.'

'Elizabeth forged it?'

'Her or a friendly lawyer. Henri was not popular.'

'His son didn't contest it?'

'He might have done but news arrived that Napoleon had escaped from Elba. Overnight he was on enemy territory. A swift exit was called for and he never returned.'

Kam uttered a single expletive.

'I'm sorry,' he apologised, 'but how do you know all this?'

'Elizabeth kept a diary.' She took it from the pocket of the long linen top she was wearing. 'She must have hidden it rather than have her own daughters know what kind of man their father was. No one would ever have known but three years ago the radiator in Grandma's room sprung a leak. The plumber had to lift the floorboards to get at the pipe and he found a package wrapped in oilcloth. Once I opened it, started reading it…'

'How did your grandmother take it?'

'I never showed it to her. She hasn't been in good health for years and I knew it would upset her and my grandfather would have burned it.'

'So you kept the secret.'

'Who would I share it with?'

Him, Kam thought. She had shared it with him.

'Are you happy to have the wedding here?' he asked.

It wasn't to be a religious ceremony but Henri's oath had been sacrilegious.

'Grandfather had left instructions that his funeral service should take place here,' she replied. 'There hadn't been a service here since my christening. I wasn't sure whether it was still consecrated even, so I asked the bishop to come and perform that service and bless it. Henri and his vile lie have been cleaned away.'

There was a string quartet playing in the choir as the congregation gathered for the wedding of Miss Agnès Elizabeth Prideaux to Kamal David Faulkner. The chapel was decorated with country casual flowers in pink and white with knots of ribbons and a bunch of pink and white balloons bearing their names and the date floating above the lectern.

Kam was sitting with his best man and business partner, Raj Chowdry, beside him. His mother, sitting behind him, touched his shoulder as if she knew that he was nervous, as only a bridegroom, suffering that last moment of uncertainty about whether his beloved would arrive, could ever be.

'She will be here.'

He placed his hand on hers then looked around.

He knew most of the people in the chapel. There were old friends from his school days, people who had helped him build his business, those who'd worked on the estate and had since retired. There were a few faces on the bride's side of the aisle he didn't recognise, school friends of Agnès, distant relatives.

The sleek, elegantly tailored man sitting with her grandmother looked vaguely familiar, but before he could put his mind to where he'd seen him before there was a rustle of activity at the rear of the chapel. A child's voice asking in a loud whisper when there would be cake provoked a ripple of laughter.

Finally the celebrant stepped forward and there was a moment of silence before the first notes of Pachelbel's 'Canon' filled the chapel.

As one, their guests rose to watch as Agnès walked, alone and unsupported, towards him, a posse of bridesmaids, being gently corralled by Suzanna, following her down the aisle.

She had no one to give her away. She was a strong woman, making her own choice as she gave herself to him, knowing that he was giving himself to her.

Strong, beautiful, a vision in white lace worn over a simple dress. There was no veil to hide her face, just the Prideaux tiara in her hair, a posy of the roses she'd named for her mother in her hand as she walked towards him.

As she reached her grandmother she stopped to kiss her cheek, give her the bouquet to hold. Then, as she straightened and saw the man standing beside her grandmother, she stilled.

In that moment he knew where he had seen that face before. On the portrait of Henri Prideaux hanging over the fireplace in the library.

The man murmured something to Agnès that only she and her grandmother could hear.

He was at her side in a step, and without a word his mother crossed the aisle and took Lady Prideaux away to sit with her.

'If you have something to say, Prideaux,' he said, 'you will have your chance to stand up and say it in front of everyone but we are here to celebrate a wedding.'

The service was a simple one. It began with the simple declaration from Agnès and from himself that they knew of no impediment to their marriage. Pierre Prideaux appeared to have thought better of interrupting the service and it continued with one of Raj's children reading *How Do I Love Thee?* by Elizabeth

Barrett Browning. Someone Agnès knew from school sang 'The Rose'.

Then it was time for their vows.

Agnès took his hands and said, 'I chose you as my friend when I was six years old, Kam Faulkner, when you were a scruffy boy and I was a lonely little girl. I chose you as my lover when I was a few weeks shy of my sixteenth birthday, too young to know that love isn't always enough. In all the time since then no one has ever touched my heart as you did then, and now that I am twenty-six I still choose you as my friend, my lover, my joy. I will choose you and choose you and choose you, Kam, with all my heart, with all my soul, with everything I have and I will still be choosing you with my dying breath.'

For a moment his throat was thick with emotion and he could do nothing but tighten his grip on her hands before gathering himself to respond.

'I had a pretty vow written for you, my lovely Agnès, but at this moment I want to make you a promise. It's not pretty, but it's my solemn vow to you and it's this. If we are not blessed with children and anything, God forbid, should happen to you, I swear that before I let Pierre Prideaux or any of his ilk step foot in Priddy Castle, I will make it your funeral pyre.'

There was an audible gasp from the congregation, followed by footsteps and the crash of the ancient oak doors as Pierre Prideaux left the chapel, but none of that mattered because Agnès was kissing him.

After a moment the celebrant cleared her throat. 'We seem to have got a little ahead of ourselves. There are a few formalities before you get to the good part.' There was a ripple of relieved laughter from the congregation as she turned to Raj and said, 'Do you have the rings?'

They exchanged rings, signed the register, then they were outside in the sunshine, a photographer doing his best to marshal them into position.

'What did he say to you?' he asked.

She shook her head. 'Nothing I'd soil my mouth with. The words of a man who has lost, Kam. You wiped them clean away with the power of your promise.'

* * *

Agnès had chosen to celebrate their wedding with a picnic in the wild part of the garden.

There was a carousel, an entertainer for the children, a conjurer moving among the crowd amusing everyone with close-up magic. And after the feasting, when the light began to fade and the fairy lights strung amongst the wild roses and honeysuckle climbing through the trees began to twinkle, there was a dance floor with a local group providing the music.

'What did you choose as a first dance?' Agnès asked as Kam took her hand and led her onto the dance floor.

'This.' One of the group handed him a guitar. 'You gave me this a long time ago asking only that one day I play a song just for you. This is it.'

He ran his fingers lightly over the strings and then he began to sing.

He sang the first verse, the chorus and then he handed the guitar to someone standing in the crowd and took her in his arms. Still singing, with everyone standing around watching them as, dancing in the dark, he spun her slowly around all their friends who had gathered to watch. And then, when the song ended, they just stood there in each other's arms and he said, 'Did I do okay?'

And, smiling, she said, 'It was…perfect.'

It was dark. Behind the castle, the party was still in full swing but down on the beach the only sound was the water lapping against the sand, the churring of a nightjar, the soft grumble of a duck.

The only light as Agnès walked out of the cave where she had left her dress, the lacy underwear expected of a bride, came from the stars and the thinnest crescent moon.

The water was cold as she waded in up to her waist then launched herself out into the creek, but Kam was waiting as she reached the little beach and walked towards him, star-silvered water streaming from her body.

'You're cold,' he said, as he took her hand. Just as he had that first time.

And she said, 'Warm me.'

* * * * *